MURDER ON *THE CANADIAN*

BOOKS BY ERIC WILSON

The Tom and Liz Austen Mysteries
Murder on The Canadian
Vancouver Nightmare
The Case of the Golden Boy
Disneyland Hostage
The Kootenay Kidnapper
Vampires of Ottawa
Spirit in the Rainforest
The Green Gables Detectives
Code Red at the Supermall
Cold Midnight in Vieux Québec
The Ice Diamond Quest
The Prairie Dog Conspiracy
The St. Andrews Werewolf
The Inuk Mountie Adventure
Escape from Big Muddy
The Emily Carr Mystery
The Ghost of Lunenburg Manor
Terror in Winnipeg
The Lost Treasure of Casa Loma
Red River Ransom

Also available by Eric Wilson
Summer of Discovery
The Unmasking of 'Ksan

MURDER ON
THE
CANADIAN

A Tom Austen Mystery
40th Anniversary Edition

ERIC WILSON

Harper*Trophy* Canada

Published by Harper*Trophy*Canada™,
an imprint of HarperCollins Publishers Ltd

First published in hardcover by Clarke, Irwin & Company, Ltd and
The Bodley Head (Canada) Ltd: 1976 First Collins paperback edition: 1983.
First HarperCollins paperback edition: 1991.
This HarperCollins trade paperback: 2016

Harper*Trophy*Canada™ is a trademark of HarperCollins Publishers Ltd

HarperCollins books may be purchased for educational, business,
or sales promotional use through our Special Markets Department.

HarperCollins Publishers Ltd
2 Bloor Street East, 20th Floor
Toronto, Ontario, Canada
M4W 1A8

www.harpercollins.ca

Library and Archives Canada Cataloguing in Publication
information is available upon request.

ISBN 978-1-44345-015-7

Printed and bound in the United States
RRD 9 8 7 6 5 4 3 2 1

Chapter illustrations: Richard Row

For Mum and Dad with love

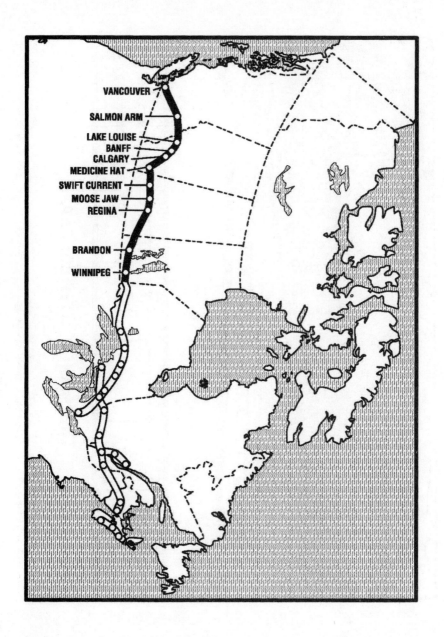

VANCOUVER
SALMON ARM
LAKE LOUISE
BANFF
CALGARY
MEDICINE HAT
SWIFT CURRENT
MOOSE JAW
REGINA
BRANDON
WINNIPEG

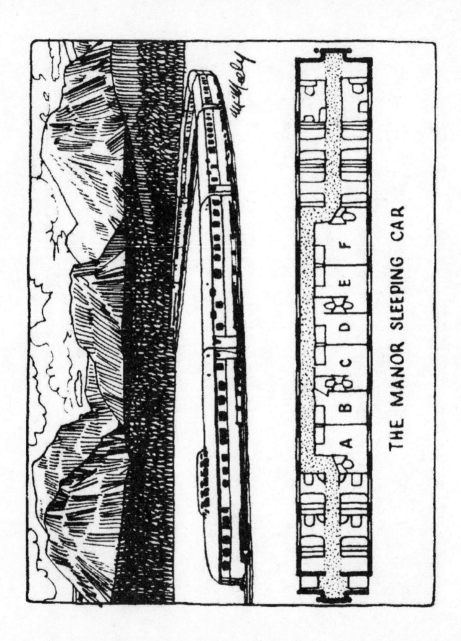

THE MANOR SLEEPING CAR

MURDER ON *THE CANADIAN*

1

The package was ticking.

A bomb. Yes, Tom was sure it must be a bomb. He studied the plain brown paper, then leaned his head close.

Tick. Tick. Tick.

Frightened, Tom looked around the crowded railway station. What to do? If he yelled "Bomb!" it might cause a panic, a rush to the doors in which women and children would be crushed underfoot.

Again, Tom studied the package which had appeared mysteriously beside his suitcase minutes ago when he'd gone to the washroom. It looked innocent, but the ticking meant it was deadly.

Tom spotted a man in a conductor's uniform across the station. He ran forward, pushing through the crowds of people waiting to board the train, and grabbed the man's arm.

"Please, sir," he said, panting, "please come quickly!"

The man looked down at Tom with huge blue eyes magnified by thick glasses. "What?" he said, cupping a hand around his ear.

"Help!" Tom said, afraid to shout there was a bomb. The man shook his head. "Can't hear you, sonny. Station too noisy."

The conductor lost interest in Tom and returned to writing on a pad. For a wild second Tom thought he should get out, save his own life, then he snatched the conductor's pad and ran.

"You little devil!" the man shouted.

Faces turned, staring at the flash of Tom's red hair as he darted past, the conductor close behind. The man was a fast runner and had almost caught Tom when he reached his suitcase.

The package was gone.

Impossible. Tom grabbed his suitcase, looking behind it for the missing bomb, and then the conductor grabbed Tom.

"You little brat!" he shouted.

Now everything was confusion. The conductor tore his notepad from Tom's hand; excited people pushed close to watch; a dog began to bark, and Tom found the bomb.

In the hands of Dietmar Oban. Yes, Tom's rival held the package, a wicked grin on his face as he pushed close among the crowd of onlookers.

Tom had been tricked, and now he knew that the ticking "bomb" was really just an old alarm clock. Feeling stupid, Tom looked up at the angry conductor.

"Please, sir," he said weakly, "I can explain everything."

"I'll have the police on you!"

"Yes, but . . ."

From above, a loudspeaker boomed: "All passengers board the train." The onlookers hesitated, hating to leave the excitement Tom had caused, then turned and shuffled away. The conductor's huge blue eyes stared down at Tom.

"No more trouble, sonny, or you'll end up behind bars."

"Yes, sir," Tom said.

He watched the conductor walk away, then whirled to grab Dietmar, but he was gone. Shaking his head, Tom picked up his suitcase and started toward the platform doors.

Happily, the excitement of the coming trip returned quickly to Tom. Reaching the platform he found a thrilling scene. Redcaps rushed past with piles of luggage, the loudspeaker buzzed with announcements, and porters in white jackets chatted together as passengers hurried by.

But the greatest thrill of all was the train. Huge, hissing steam, its stainless steel body gleaming under the platform lights, The Canadian lay like a giant along the tracks, waiting impatiently to hurl itself forward into the coming adventure. Tom shivered with the beauty of the train. He wanted to stand and stare, but the diesel's whistle blasted and he hurried to the nearest car.

"Ticket, please," a porter said, the words whistling through a gap between his front teeth. Tom studied the old man's face, hoping he would be a friend on the trip.

"I'll take that, sir," the porter said, reaching for Tom's suitcase and leading the way up into the car. They pushed inside through a door marked Sherwood Manor, passed some tiny roomettes, then walked along a corridor with a row of blue doors.

"What's in there?" Tom asked the porter.

"Bedrooms," he answered, "for folks with money."

Around a bend they came to seats facing each other in pairs. The porter shoved Tom's suitcase under a seat.

"This is your place," he said. "When we leave Winnipeg, I'll pull these two seats together and make them into a bed. Have a pleasant journey, Mr. Austen."

Tom smiled at the porter, then looked across the aisle at a man and woman who sat in another pair of seats.

"Hello, young fellow," said the man, whose thumbs were hooked inside wide suspenders, "where you bound?"

"British Columbia. I'm going to spend the summer with my grandparents."

The woman held out a large tin. "Have one of my cookies?" she asked, smiling at Tom.

"Yes, please."

"Your friend ate four."

"My friend?"

"The boy you're travelling with." She pointed under Tom's seat. " There's his suitcase, beside yours."

"Oh no," Tom whispered to himself, afraid to look. He knelt down beside the suitcase, and shuddered when he read the label: Dietmar Oban.

The woman was beaming as Tom stood up. "Such a nice boy," she said. "A bit thin, but my chocolate chip cookies will soon build him up."

What unbelievably bad luck, trapped with Dietmar Oban! A beautiful trip ruined, but at least he could start it by getting Dietmar for that bomb trick. Tom turned to the woman.

"Which way did the dirty rat go?" he demanded.

A frown crossed the woman's face, and she firmly closed the lid of the cookie tin before saying coldly, "To the dome."

"Thanks." Tom didn't know what the dome was, but it was no use asking the woman anything more. Seeing a door in the end of the car, he went through it, crossed a narrow platform, and pushed open a second door. In this car people sat drinking coffee at tiny tables; beyond them, a flight of carpeted stairs led up into darkness.

Up into the dome?

Tom climbed up cautiously, afraid of what the darkness might hold, but he relaxed when he found two long rows of seats surrounded by huge, curved windows. Through these windows, he could see the lights of the station and, straight above, the night sky. Neat!

And there was a bonus: Dietmar Oban was in one of the seats. Tom tiptoed forward, slipped into the seat beside Dietmar, and grabbed his arm.

"You fink," Tom hissed, "I've got you."

Dietmar jumped, and turned to Tom with wide eyes. "Take it easy, Austen, it was just a joke."

"I ought to rub you out," Tom said, squeezing his rival's skinny arm.

"Listen, Austen, I can give you a mystery to solve."

"You're lying, to save your skin."

"I'm not. Let go of my arm, and I'll tell you."

Tom hesitated, gave a final squeeze that made Dietmar wince, then let him go. A mystery was better than revenge any day.

"What is it?" Tom asked. "Shake your news and pour it out."

Dietmar laughed. "You and your detective talk, Austen. You sound nuts."

"Just give me the facts, Oban."

Dietmar pointed to a man sitting across the dome car. "See that guy?"

"Yeah." The man's grey hair and dark business suit looked ordinary enough. "What about him?"

"Go sit beside him, and you'll see the mystery."

Tom got out of his seat, walked along the narrow

aisle and sat beside the man. Wanting to avoid suspicion, he yawned and stretched his arms, then pretended to fall asleep. He counted to thirty in his head,
then opened his eyes in a narrow slit: there was a
handcuff on the man's wrist!

Tom gasped, and the man turned toward him, but
Tom pretended to be mumbling in his sleep and began
to snore gently. He waited for the man to relax, then
opened his eyes again. Yes, a handcuff was attached
to the man's wrist, then a short chain ran to a second
handcuff, which was locked to the handle of a black
attaché case resting on the man's lap. Tom could see a
small combination lock on the case, but there was no
indication of what might be inside.

Tom pretended to wake up slowly, smacking his
lips and stretching his arms, then he slid out of the
seat and returned to Dietmar's side.

"I saw that guy come up here," Dietmar whispered, "and I figured you'd want to investigate him."

Tom looked suspiciously at Dietmar. "You making
fun of me?"

"No, I mean it. I know you want to solve crimes
when you grow up. What is it you want to be?"

"A gumshoe. That's a detective, like the Hardy
Boys."

"Well, gumboot, now you've got a real puzzle on your hands."

Tom shot a dirty look at Dietmar. The most sarcastic kid in Queenston School, and here he was sharing Tom's train trip. Still, he had found a good mystery to solve.

"You know what I figure?" Tom whispered.

"What?"

"That guy's a jewel thief."

Dietmar leaned forward to study the man. "I think you're right. He looks just like a thief I saw on a TV mystery."

"He's got his tools in that attaché case. A skeleton key for opening bedroom doors and a blowtorch to open safes. He's got the case handcuffed to his wrist so no one can open it accidentally and find out he's a thief."

"What are you going to do?"

"Keep him under surveillance. He may be planning to rob some rich people during the trip."

Music had been flowing like thick syrup from a speaker in the front of the dome car. Now it stopped, and a man's voice came out: "Good evening, ladies and gentlemen. *The Canadian* is ready to depart. We hope you enjoy your journey." More music, then the car shook as the big diesel engine started forward.

"Look," Tom said, pointing through a window at the front of the dome, "you can see the whole train."

Both boys stood up to get a better view along the backs of stainless steel cars to the engine, which sent spurts of exhaust smoke into the air as it strained against the tremendous weight of the train. Slowly, slowly, *The Canadian* rolled forward and then began to pick up speed.

Ahead, signal lights flashed from green to red as the engine rumbled past, its steel wheels banging through a series of switches; to each side, rows of boxcars stood in black lines, beyond them the lights of the city. Tom and Dietmar remained on their feet, looking out the big windows, until the train left Winnipeg behind and slipped into the vast darkness of the prairie.

Tom trembled. "It's so black out here," he whispered. "It's creepy."

Dietmar laughed. "The great detective, afraid of the dark."

Tom blushed, and was about to slug Dietmar, when something strange caught his eye. The mysterious man, hearing Dietmar say "detective," had turned in their direction and now his eyes were staring at Tom. Then, suddenly, he swung out of his seat and quickly left the dome, the chain at his wrist clinking softly as he passed the two boys.

2

"You banana," Tom whispered, "now he knows I'm a detective."

"Are you going to tail him?"

"I'd better."

Tom ran quickly down the stairs. Looking through the windows of the connecting doors, he saw the man standing in the sleeping-car, talking to the old porter. As Tom watched, the porter shook his head; the man, looking angry, turned and disappeared in the direction of the corridor with the blue bedroom doors.

Tom hurried into the sleeping-car. "Excuse me, sir," he said to the porter, "where can I find that man you just spoke to?"

"Bedroom A," the porter said, then looked carefully at Tom. "Why?"

"Oh, he, uh, dropped something."

The porter studied Tom's face, then returned to preparing berths for the night. Tom walked on slowly, uncertain how Frank and Joe Hardy would handle this case, then decided to wait around and hope for a break. Perhaps he could catch a glimpse of burglar tools.

Tom saw no sign of the man in the long corridor, but at the far end was the most beautiful woman he had ever seen. Tom stopped, staring, as the woman approached, one arm supporting a man who was very drunk.

Neither seemed to notice Tom as they came slowly forward, being thrown back and forth by the motion of the speeding train. Tom glanced for a moment at the man's bloodshot eyes, then looked with awe at the woman's shining blond hair and violet-coloured eyes. She was marvellous.

Reaching a bedroom door, the woman turned the handle and helped the man inside. The door closed, and again the corridor was empty.

Slowly, Tom walked forward, pausing outside the couple's door when he heard the mutter of voices. Unable to make out the words, he walked on to Bedroom A, but the door was closed. Anyway Tom had lost interest for the moment in the man with the handcuffs. Tom was in love.

He couldn't get the woman out of his mind, the colour of her eyes, the softness of her hair, the creamy smoothness of her skin. Who was she? Returning along the corridor, Tom stopped again outside the couple's door, then rushed to tell Dietmar.

"Guess what?" he said, sitting down. "There's a beautiful woman in our car!"

Dietmar laughed. "That cookie-woman? She's beautiful like Godzilla the Hun is beautiful."

"No, a woman in Bedroom C. She's got violet eyes, and she's wearing a gold necklace. I wonder who she is?"

"Cinderella. She turns into a prune at midnight."

Dietmar's sarcasm was spoiling Tom's memory of the woman. He closed his eyes, dreaming of her face, then opened them in surprise when there was a flash of light.

"What was that?"

"Lightning," Dietmar said, pointing out the window. "Over there."

At first Tom could see only blackness, then a

streak of pure white ripped across the sky, twisting and exploding in all directions. A delicate pattern of jagged light hung for a moment in the air, then died.

"That's lovely," Tom said.

Dietmar nodded. Together they watched the sky, and were rewarded with another burst of white light. It was followed by a rumble of thunder and the long moan of the diesel's whistle.

"What a creepy sound," Tom said. "Do you know any ghost stories?"

"Nope."

Another streak of lightning trembled across the night sky, bright in Tom's eyes. "Bet you don't know how to kill a werewolf," he said.

"Sure I do. You shove a silver cross in its face."

"That doesn't kill it," Tom said. He glanced up as the cookie-woman came along the aisle and took the seat in front of the boys, then lowered his voice to a whisper, "You drive a stake through its heart."

"A steak? What a waste of good food."

"No, you idiot! You try to catch the werewolf asleep in its coffin, and jab a wooden stake through its heart."

The cookie-woman turned to look at Tom as he lifted his hands to demonstrate the powerful blow needed to kill a werewolf.

"That's a very silly thing to talk about," she said. "Anyway, I'm sure it's long past your bedtime."

"We're on a holiday, having fun," Tom said. "At least, we were until a minute ago."

The cookie-woman looked at Tom with distaste, then turned to face forward.

"So, as I was saying," Tom said after a moment, winking at Dietmar, "I think for fun we should release my snakes tonight while everyone is sleeping."

The cookie-woman shifted uncomfortably in her seat, and Dietmar grinned. "Gosh, Tom," he said innocently, "what if a rattlesnake bites someone, and they die?"

"I didn't bring my rattlers this trip, just the big garter snakes. You know, those long green slimy ones that like to slip into bed and curl up around your feet."

"You sure they won't bite?"

"Not unless someone gets scared. Then they might give the person a nip with their fangs, but the bite only makes your body swell up for a couple of days."

Suddenly, the cookie-woman's head whipped around and she stared fiercely at Tom. There was a long silence while Tom stared back at her, trying to keep a straight face, then he heard Dietmar giggle and burst into laughter.

"I knew you were fooling!" the cookie-woman said, sounding both relieved and angry. Standing up, she shook her finger in Tom's face. "You're a very naughty little boy."

Fighting back his laughter, Tom watched the woman leave the dome, then turned to Dietmar and they both howled. When they had finished laughing, and wiped their eyes, they told each other the story and laughed some more. Then they calmed down and sat watching the thunderstorm light up the prairie until finally Dietmar yawned.

"I'm for bed," he said, stretching his arms.

"Good idea."

Tom led the way to their sleeping-car, where heavy curtains hung along both sides of the narrow corridor. It was dark, the only lights glowing softly at their feet. Dietmar turned to Tom, his face worried.

"Where'd our seats go?" he asked.

"The porter turned them into beds for the night," Tom said. "Haven't you travelled on a train before?"

"Nope."

"Well stick with me, Oban, and I'll show you around." Tom reached for a pair of curtains and began to undo some large buttons. "This is my berth."

Tom threw open the curtains, and there was a

shriek. He looked inside, saw the cookie-woman in a nightdress, and jerked the curtains closed. His face on fire, he turned to Dietmar.

"Wrong berth."

Dietmar was grinning. "Wait till I tell the kids at school!"

Tom shook his fist under Dietmar's nose. "Do it, and you'll be eating a knuckle sandwich."

Above their heads, curtains were yanked open and the cookie-woman's husband looked out. "Pipe down, you kids. Decent people are trying to sleep."

"We can't find our berths," Tom said.

The man pointed at a ladder hidden in the folds of some curtains. "One of you climb up there. The other sleeps below."

"Oh boy!" Tom and Dietmar said together. "A ladder!"

They both made a grab for the ladder, but Dietmar was closer and went up it like a monkey. "See you tomorrow," he said, crawling into the berth.

Annoyed that Dietmar had the best berth, Tom opened the lower curtains. He slipped off his shoes, climbed on to the bed and closed the curtains.

It was like being in a dark cave. Tom found a switch and clicked on a tiny blue lamp, then looked around. A blind covered the window, the upper berth stretched just above his head, and the blue light shone on two soft pillows, white sheets and blankets. Anxious to try the bed, Tom made a pile of his clothes, adjusted the pillows, and crawled between the crisp sheets.

Beautiful. Tom stretched his arms, feeling luxurious, and reached to open the blind. Outside, the night was solid black except for three red lights on a distant radio tower. The train went around a bend, and Tom could see the diesel's powerful headlight slicing a path through the night.

He was falling asleep. What rotten luck, just when he wanted to treasure the feeling of lying in bed with the whole world flying by outside. Tom opened his eyes wide, watched as the train passed a farmhouse with a yellow light shining from a window, and fell sound asleep.

He dreamed of a conductor with huge blue eyes, offering a cookie that turned into a bomb and exploded, filling the air with violet smoke that became violet eyes smiling at Tom as a bedroom door opened and a man wearing a silver cross slipped out, reaching long cold fingers for Tom's throat.

◇◇◇◇◇◇

A whistle shrieked, the bed threw Tom back and forth, and he sat up with sweat on his face. Who was the man? Was he real, or a dream? Again the whistle blew, and Tom looked out the window, realizing it had been a nightmare.

The train was slowing down. Tom could see rows of tracks, a throbbing yard engine, red and green lights on switches, then a long platform with people standing around looking sleepy. Brakes squealing, the train stopped beside a station marked BRANDON.

Quickly, Tom pulled on his clothes, anxious to get off the train and explore. He opened the curtains, stepped into the corridor, and saw Dietmar coming down the ladder.

"Hi," Tom said. "Want to go poke around this station?"

"Where are we?"

"Brandon. Didn't you see the sign from your window?"

"What window? All I've got is a steel wall."

"Gee, that's too bad," Tom said, grinning. "I guess you grabbed the ladder too fast."

Walking through the car, Tom stopped outside Bedroom C when he heard a man's voice shouting angry words. Was that drunk abusing his beautiful wife? Tom looked around, ready to go for help, but he relaxed when he heard the woman laugh.

"Come on!" Dietmar called impatiently from the end of the corridor.

"Okay, okay." Tom looked at the blue bedroom door, memorizing the sound of the woman's silvery laughter, before going reluctantly to join Dietmar.

Outside, the summer night was warm. Tom and Dietmar walked along the platform to the baggage car, where they watched men tossing mailbags into the back of a truck, then continued ahead to the engine. Tom felt small as he stood looking up at its powerful steel body, the huge headlight and curved windscreen.

"I'd love to drive one of those," he said to Dietmar.

"You'd make a good driver."

"Why?" Tom asked, pleased.

"Because you drive me crazy." Dietmar turned and ran, laughing. Tom chased him down the platform, caught him and threatened to throw him under the train. As they wrestled, a hand touched Tom's shoulder.

"Excuse me, young man," an old cracked voice said. "I'd like some help."

Tom let go of Dietmar and looked at an old woman

leaning on a cane, a shawl around her stooped shoulders. Without waiting for them to speak, she crooked her finger at the boys.

"Come along," she ordered, turning to hobble across the platform.

"I'll bet she's a retired school teacher," Tom whispered to Dietmar. "Come on, let's give her a hand."

Tom and Dietmar followed the woman to a taxi, where she pointed with her cane at a pile of suitcases. "These are my bags," she said. "Help the driver with them, and I'll give you both a tip."

The driver, a tall man with a cap stuck on the back of his head, grinned at the boys and winked. He handed them some suitcases, and they walked slowly behind the old lady to the train.

Other passengers were also boarding at Brandon, and Tom was pushed to one side by a short, fat man who arrogantly waved a ticket in the porter's face and climbed quickly aboard. The porter shook his head, muttering, as he took the old lady's ticket.

"I tell you," he said, "some folks make a man tired."

The old lady made a clucking noise with her mouth. "Let me give you some fudge," she said, reaching into her handbag and handing him a sticky brown piece.

The porter put it in his mouth, licked his fingers and helped the old lady up the steps. Tom, Dietmar and the taxi driver struggled along behind with the suitcases, which banged against the narrow walls of the sleeping-car.

The porter had just opened a bedroom door for the old lady when a loud voice was heard swearing. This was followed by silence, then angry shouts. Everyone turned to stare, wondering what was happening behind the door to Bedroom C.

3

The porter was the first to act.

Quickly, he walked to the bedroom door and knocked. The shouting stopped, then a man's voice yelled, "Go away!"

Again the porter knocked, but there was no reply. Down the corridor, the door to Bedroom A opened and the greying man stepped out, the attaché case still linked to his wrist.

"What's going on?" he asked.

"Nothing, sir," the porter replied. "Please go back to sleep."

For the first time, Tom noticed the greying man was still fully clothed, even though it was late at night and other passengers were asleep. As Tom thought about this strange fact, something even stranger happened: the short, fat man who'd pushed aboard the train a few minutes ago now opened the door of Bedroom B and came out, wearing pyjamas.

How could he have changed so quickly? Puzzled, Tom watched as the two men glanced at each other, seemed about to speak, then went into their bedrooms and closed the doors.

At the same moment, the door to Bedroom C was thrown open. The beautiful woman, dressed in a soft pink robe, looked out angrily at the porter.

"Why are you knocking?" she demanded.

"Excuse me, ma'am," the porter said, "but we heard a fight. We were concerned for your safety."

"Mind your own business," the woman said, closing the door in the porter's face.

Tom was shocked at the woman's rudeness. He looked at the porter's embarrassed face, feeling sorry for the man. The old lady, clucking, reached into her handbag for more fudge.

"Mercy!" she said, passing it to the porter. "I hope this won't be an unpleasant trip."

"No, ma'am," he said. "If necessary, I'll take action against that couple. They won't bother you, don't worry."

Tom put down the suitcases outside the old lady's bedroom and was walking away with Dietmar when she called out, "Just a minute!"

Tom turned, and saw her opening her handbag. She reached inside and took out two nickels.

"Here you are," she said, handing each boy a coin, "thank you for your assistance."

Dietmar stared down at the nickel, unable to hide his disgust, then looked cheekily at the old lady. "How about some fudge?"

"Certainly not," she said. "It's bad for your teeth."

"So are knuckle sandwiches," Dietmar said. "Maybe I'll treat you to one."

"Goodness gracious!" the old lady said, watching Dietmar walk angrily away. "What a rude little boy. This train is full of hooligans."

Tom smiled at her. "Thanks for the money, ma'am. Have a nice trip."

The old lady beamed. "That's better! Here you are, young man, a little treat."

A piece of fudge was produced, and Tom walked away, chewing happily. He crawled into his bed, watched the activity on the platform for awhile, then fell into a deep sleep.

◇◇◇◇◇◇

Morning came with a *bing bong bing*. Tom felt sunshine on his face, opened his eyes, and again heard the curious sound: *bing bong bing*. It was followed by a man's voice announcing, "Breakfast is served."

The voice died away, and Tom sat up. He looked out the window at fields of young green wheat, swaying gently under a wind that blew toward the horizon. He began to pull on his clothes. He was hungry!

Tom opened his curtains and found Dietmar sitting on the edge of the upper berth, feet dangling.

"Hi," Tom said. "What was that weird sound?"

"A xylophone. Some guy walked by playing it, and hollering 'breakfast.'"

"Wait for me, and I'll go with you." Tom went into the washroom at the end of the corridor, then joined Dietmar and they walked through the train to the dining-car. As they opened the door, the smell of bacon and eggs came to their noses.

"I could eat a horse," Tom said.

"How about an old bat? Like that one who gave us a nickel."

Tom laughed. "She gave me some fudge, too."
"You're lying."

Tom shook his head. He led the way into a room full of sunshine glistening on white tablecloths, on which were silver, glasses and flowers. Waiters hurried back and forth with big trays full of food for the passengers, who chatted together or looked out the windows.

A smiling man approached. "Good morning," he said. "Would you like breakfast?"

"Yes, please," Tom answered.

"This way." The steward led them through the car to a table for four, where he held out a chair for Tom, then the one beside it for Dietmar. He gave them the menu and smiled again. "*Bon appétit.*"

"What did he say?" Dietmar whispered, when the steward was gone.

Tom shrugged. He looked at the silver and china, which tinkled together with the train's motion, then opened the menu. "Oh no!" he said. "It's all in French."

"*Jus de fruits,*" Dietmar read, struggling with the words. "Does that mean there's just fruit for breakfast?"

"Here's the English," Tom said, pointing to another part of the menu. "I'm having Rice Krispies with cream, toast and coffee."

"I hate coffee."

"So do I, actually, but it looks good written on the menu." Tom looked at a pad and pencil which the smiling steward had left on the table. "I think we have to write our order here."

As Tom bent over the order pad, the smell of perfume came to his nose. His heart beating with excitement, he looked up and saw the beautiful woman approaching. Unable to believe his luck, Tom watched the steward lead her straight to his table and hold out a chair; he then put the woman's husband opposite Dietmar, took Tom's order, and walked away.

The woman glanced at Tom, and his face went red. Furious with himself, he looked down and pretended to study the menu.

"*Parlez-vous français?*" the woman's husband said.

Tom looked up. "What?"

The man smiled. "I asked if you speak French. I noticed you reading the French part of the menu."

"Oh," Tom said, his face going redder as he felt the woman's eyes staring. "Oh, French, yes, well, I mean . . . *oui.*"

Dietmar laughed. "Austen hasn't even learned to talk English yet. In fact, he still wears diapers."

The woman laughed at the joke, and Tom aimed a kick sideways at Dietmar but missed. The man held out his hand to Tom. "My name is Richard Saks," he said. "This is my wife, Catherine."

Tom shook the man's hand, liking his face now that he wasn't drunk. He looked at his dark-brown hair and moustache, then turned shyly to the woman. "I'm Tom Austen," he said, "and this is Dietmar Oban."

"Oh." The woman yawned, then opened her handbag and took out a gold case and a cigarette holder. Putting in a cigarette, she lifted the long, elegant holder to her lips.

"What will you have, princess?" Richard Saks asked his wife.

"Coffee."

Tom smiled to himself, pleased that he had also ordered coffee. When the woman turned to look out the window he studied the flickering diamonds on her fingers, the string of pearls over her black sweater and the makeup around her lovely eyes.

"Do you know if those are real pearls?" he asked.

Catherine Saks looked at Tom, startled. "What?"

"I can test your pearls by rubbing them against my teeth. If they're phony, they slip; if they're real, they grate." Tom hesitated, feeling foolish under the stare from the violet eyes, then explained, "I read that in a detective handbook."

"Do you think I would wear phony pearls?"

Catherine Saks demanded, touching the pearls with her sharp-pointed fingernails.

"No, I . . . I . . ."

"Don't mind old Carrot Top," Dietmar said. "He thinks he's a Hardy Boy."

"I read all their books when I was a kid," Richard Saks said. "They're terrific."

Tom smiled at the man, feeling grateful. A waiter arrived with the Rice Krispies, and Tom poured cream from a silver jug among them, feeling hungry as they crackled.

Not wanting to stare at the beauty of Catherine Saks, Tom looked out the window at the fields that rolled away toward a distant grain elevator. The train roared past a blue pond, and a cluster of tiny black birds scrambled into the air from an old fence half-buried in the water. Tom felt good, and was trying to find the courage to speak to Catherine Saks when Dietmar looked at her.

"Are you a model?" he asked.

"No," Catherine Saks said, smiling. "Why do you ask?"

"Because you're so beautiful."

Catherine Saks glowed as she looked at Dietmar. "Do you think so? You're very flattering. In fact, I was once in the movies."

"Wow," Dietmar said, "a movie star!"

"Well, not exactly a star. But I had several lines in a movie called *My Little Pussycat*. Have you seen it on TV?"

"Uh, sure," Dietmar said. "You were great!"

Tom looked at Dietmar, knowing he was lying, and hating him for finding it so easy to talk to Catherine Saks.

"Were you in Hollywood?" Tom asked.

"Yes," Catherine Saks answered, still looking at Dietmar. "But I got sick of it, and returned home to Winnipeg with a friend of mine, who'd also been acting in Hollywood."

"They both got jobs in my bank," Richard Saks said, "and it wasn't long before Catherine and I fell in love." He looked at his wife with adoration, but Tom didn't think there was much love in the glance she tossed him in return.

"Do you miss being a star?" Dietmar asked.

"You bet," Catherine Saks answered. She stared off into space for a minute, then said softly, "If I was free again, I'd go straight back to Hollywood."

As she said this, Tom was looking at Richard Saks, and saw a look of pain cross the man's face. No wonder he drank, when he knew his wife wanted to be free of their marriage.

"Where are you going?" Tom asked Richard Saks, trying to change the subject.

"To Victoria," the man answered, his face brightening. "Catherine needs a holiday, she's been under such a strain lately."

"Why?" Tom asked.

"It's nothing," Catherine Saks said, in a tone which indicated it was none of Tom's business.

Richard Saks put his arm around his wife. "Now don't you worry about it, princess," he said, giving her a hug which made her stiffen.

Tom was getting sick of Catherine Saks. He looked down at the coffee which a waiter had brought and lifted the cup, but it tasted bitter. Standing up, he smiled at Richard Saks and left the table. Dietmar and Catherine Saks could spend the whole day gazing at each other for all he cared.

"Your bill, sir," the smiling steward said, holding out his hand.

"Oh, yeah." As Tom took some money from his pocket, he saw the short, fat man cross from another table and speak to Catherine Saks. Smiling at how jealous Dietmar looked, Tom left the dining-car.

4

In the next sleeping-car, one of the bedroom doors was open. Tom looked inside and saw a young porter pulling sheets off the bed.

"Hi," Tom said, "may I see what a bedroom looks like?"

"Certainly," the porter said. He was very tall, and smiled at Tom through glasses with black frames. "I'm Dermot."

Tom gave his own name and shook Dermot's hand, then looked at a picture on the wall of a river bubbling through rapids. There was a sink with a wrap-around mirror and iced-water tap, a speaker for music and a tiny room with a toilet. "Aren't there any chairs?"

"Sure are," Dermot answered, folding the bed into the wall and revealing two squashed chairs. With a quick motion he pulled them up into their proper shape.

"Neat!" Tom said, sitting down. "Are you a university student?"

"That's right. This is my summer job."

"I'd like to do that when I'm older. Is it fun?"

"It certainly is. And you meet some strange people, like that old porter in your car."

"What's strange about him?" Tom asked.

"They say he was a professional boxer, but he was hit so hard in a fight that he was in a coma for months. When he woke up, his mind was unbalanced."

"What do you mean?"

"I hear he has fits of violent temper, when he loses control of himself. Apparently he had a fight with a conductor and threw him out the door of a speeding train."

"Wow," Tom said, feeling his hair stand on end. "That's horrible."

"Well, I don't know if it's true, but I'm always very polite around that fellow." Dermot smiled at Tom. "Well, I'd better get back to work."

"Oh, sure," Tom said, standing up. He went slowly

into the corridor, feeling so upset that he forgot to thank Dermot. What if that old man grabbed him in the middle of the night and tossed him off the train? The thought made Tom shudder, and he wondered if he should secretly trade berths with Dietmar so the porter would grab the wrong guy.

Fortunately, the old man wasn't around when Tom got to his sleeping-car. The berths had disappeared, and Tom sat down in the sunshine, letting the warmth ease his worry. Across the aisle, the cookie-woman sniffed and made a big production of putting away her tin of cookies.

Looking out the window, Tom watched the train approach a small group of trees. In their shade a horse was munching grass while its tail flicked away flies. Then a little wooden house appeared and Tom saw a girl sitting on the front steps, the wind blowing her hair. As the train passed, she raised her hand in a wave, and Tom was sure she smiled at him.

Then she was gone. Tom leaned against the glass, trying to see her again, but the little house had disappeared. He sat back in his seat, wondering who the girl was, feeling both sad and happy they had shared that one moment together.

Dietmar was coming. Tom heard his voice in the

corridor, talking to Catherine Saks, and decided he didn't feel like being sociable. He closed his eyes, pretending to be asleep, and within a few minutes was no longer pretending.

When Tom woke up, he got out *The Sinister Signpost* and a package of Dubble Bubble. After a good read, he and Dietmar had a cheeseburger in the small restaurant under the dome, then climbed upstairs and chatted happily as they watched the view.

◇◇◇◇◇◇

Getting on and off the train to explore the stations where it stopped gave Tom and Dietmar an appetite and they ate a big dinner of sugar-cured ham steak, then walked to the rear of the train for the evening bingo game.

It was held in the observation car, and everyone Tom knew seemed to be there. The first person he saw was the cookie-woman, who made a point of only saying hello to Dietmar; beside her sat the short, fat man, his shoulders sprinkled with dandruff.

Tom's heart fell when he saw those two people, but he cheered up when he spotted the old lady and she beckoned him to an empty chair at her side. As he walked between the chairs which faced each other across the observation car, Tom saw the man with the attaché case, his eyes studying Tom's face.

Pretending he didn't notice the man's stare, Tom sat down and smiled at the old lady. The evening sun made her white hair look attractive, but Tom didn't much like the powder, rouge and lipstick which she had applied to her face in thick gobs.

"Hi," he said. "I'm Tom Austen."

"And I'm Mrs. Ruggles," the old lady said, smiling.

"Any more fudge?" he asked.

"Naughty boy," the old lady said, wagging a finger. "Mustn't spoil your appetite."

"I've already had dinner," Tom protested.

"Then you'll spoil your breakfast."

Dietmar, who had taken a chair across from them, shook his head. "Cheapskate," he muttered.

Ignoring Dietmar, Mrs. Ruggles opened her handbag and took out a paper bag. She handed a piece of fudge to Tom, then offered the bag to the man with the attaché case, who sat to her left.

"Thank you," he said, reaching in and selecting a large piece.

Mrs. Ruggles got out of her chair and hobbled along the aisle, offering fudge to everyone, smiling happily as they exclaimed about its qualities.

Reaching Dietmar, she held out the bag and he helped himself.

"You don't mind eating a cheapskate's fudge?" Mrs. Ruggles asked.

Dietmar blushed. It was the first time Tom had ever seen Dietmar embarrassed, and it made him feel great. Grinning, he turned to look out the window; as he did, he noticed the man with the attaché case was still staring.

This time Tom returned the stare and the man looked away. What was going on? Puzzled, Tom watched the evening sun drop out of sight, leaving behind a sky beautifully streaked with reds and oranges and yellows.

"Take your cards for bingo," a voice said.

Tom turned and saw Dermot. Smiling, the tall young porter handed bingo cards around and then set up a wire cage containing numbered ping-pong balls. He spun the cage, and removed a ball.

"Under the B, number nine," Dermot announced. "Do we have a winner?"

Everyone laughed. As the porter spun the cage again, there was a commotion from the bar, which was a separate room in the front of the car.

"Under the 0, number sixty-five," Dermot said, raising his voice above the noise from the bar.

There was an angry shout, and Tom recognized the voice of Richard Saks. "Get out of here!" the man yelled. "I hate the sight of you!"

Dermot tried to carry on, bravely calling another number, but everyone was staring toward the bar. There was a pause, then the watchers were rewarded with the sight of Catherine Saks stalking down the corridor and out of the car.

"It's that blond hussy," the cookie-woman said to her husband. "I told you she's a troublemaker."

The short, fat man gave her a dirty look. "I think she's lovely," he said.

"I agree," Dietmar said, then looked at the cookie-woman. "Besides, she was a movie star, and I bet you never were."

Before the cookie-woman could express her opinion of movie stars, Mrs. Ruggles looked at Dietmar in surprise. "A movie star? Who said so?"

"She did."

Mrs. Ruggles chuckled, and shook her head. "Some star. She had five lines in one movie."

"At least she's not a cheapskate!" Dietmar jumped up, and threw his bingo card on the floor. "I'm getting out of this dump."

"Mercy!" Mrs. Ruggles said, fanning her face with

her card. "Why is everyone so upset tonight? Is there a full moon?"

"I'll tell you what's caused the trouble," the man with the attaché case said. "It's that drunk, Saks. The man is no good."

"How do you know his name?" Tom asked.

The question seemed to surprise the man. "Why, there was an article in the newspaper, on the social page. Saying that Mr. and Mrs. Richard Saks were planning a holiday in Vancouver."

"Victoria," Tom said, watching the man's face closely. "Not Vancouver."

"Oh, well, my mistake."

Dermot spun the wire cage vigorously. "Ladies and gentlemen, can we get back to business? I've many wonderful prizes to give away, like a weekend for two in beautiful Iceburg Inlet."

The short, fat man stood up. "I'm sick of this," he said, putting down his card and leaving the car.

"Excuse me for living," Dermot said, his voice bitter.

"Gracious!" Mrs. Ruggles looked around at the other passengers. "I don't know about you people, but all this tension is hard on my nerves."

"I'm sorry, ma'am," Dermot said, then smiled. "Come on, everyone, let's have fun!"

The game proceeded without further interruption, and Tom was pleased for Mrs. Ruggles when she waved her card in excitement, and called "Bingo!" She accepted a paperback book as her prize, and insisted Dermot take two pieces of fudge in return, then stood up.

"Always quit when you're ahead," she said, reaching for her cane. "Good night, everyone."

Mrs. Ruggles wobbled along the car, the rocking motion of the train adding to her difficulties in walking. Dermot waited politely for her to leave, then announced another game.

Tom moved to Mrs. Ruggles' chair, and looked at the mysterious man. "What's in your attaché case?" he asked.

The man turned to Tom, hesitated, then smiled. "You won't believe this, but there's only paper in my case."

The man was right. Tom didn't believe that story for one minute. He studied the case, and the silver chain of the handcuffs. "It must be pretty valuable paper."

"It could be worth a million dollars."

Tom nodded his head, pretending to be impressed. He knew the man was lying, but he couldn't think of any more questions that might help to dig out the truth. He had a lot to learn before he could be a pro like Frank and Joe Hardy.

"Under the N, number thirty-eight."

Tom stayed for several games without winning, and his eyes began to feel heavy. Looking out the window at the night made him feel lonely.

Yawning, Tom stood up. He thanked Dermot for the bingo and walked through the car, glancing in to the bar to see if Richard Saks was still there.

The man sat at a small table, face flushed, eyes red. He looked at Tom and lifted a shaky hand. "Hello, little chum," he said, his voice thick.

"Hi," Tom said. "How are you?"

"Not so hot, little chum. How're you?"

"Okay. I lost at bingo."

"Another loser," Richard Saks said, shaking his head. He lifted his glass and drank, but it only seemed to make him sadder. "Take my advice, little chum, and never marry a beautiful woman."

"Yes, sir," Tom said. "Well, good night."

"It won't be for me," Richard Saks said unhappily, looking down at his glass.

Tom walked slowly through the train. The encounter with Richard Saks had deepened his sense of loneliness, and he was glad to reach his car. As he crawled between the clean white sheets of his bed, Tom felt a bit better, but then the whistle moaned out of the black night and he fell into an unhappy sleep.

It was broken by a scream.

Tom sat up in bed, horrified by the sound. It came again, a shriek of terrible anguish. Tom pulled on his jeans and ripped open the curtains of his berth. All was quiet in the corridor, and for a moment he thought he'd had a nightmare, but then the cookie-woman's face appeared between her curtains.

"What was that ghastly sound?" she said, her face white.

"I don't know," Tom answered. "I'll find out."

Again there was a shriek, followed by deep sobs, and Tom ran toward the sound. Rounding the bend into the bedroom corridor, he stopped and stared in horror. Straight ahead was Richard Saks, holding a knife smeared red with blood!

5

Richard Saks was crying.

"My princess," he sobbed. "My princess is dead."

Tears running down his face, Richard Saks looked at the bloody knife and, for a terrible moment, Tom thought he was about to kill himself. But then he dropped the knife and leaned his face against the corridor wall, moaning.

His heart pounding, Tom walked closer. As he did, he saw that the door of Mrs. Ruggles' bedroom was open. Stepping inside, Tom saw her leaning on her cane, face frozen by shock.

"Ma'am?" Tom said. "Are you all right?"

Mrs. Ruggles shuddered. "Thank God help has

come," she whispered. "I screamed and screamed. Please, help that poor woman."

Tom nodded. As he did, there was the sound of running feet in the corridor and a confusion of shouting. Tom turned, and saw the old porter grab Richard Saks and wrestle him to the floor. Then the short, fat man leaned over Richard Saks and slapped him across the face.

"You madman!" he yelled. "What have you done?"

The husband of the cookie-woman, wearing a dressing-gown over his long underwear, ran to the door of Bedroom C and looked inside. "My God," he said, his voice shaking, "it's horrible."

Tom tried to get closer, but the man closed the door and looked down at Richard Saks. "You deserve to die!" he shouted. "How could you kill a defenceless woman?"

"No," Richard Saks whispered. His face was grey, with red marks where he had been slapped. "No, no."

By now the corridor was full of passengers, pushing and straining to see what had happened. Realizing that Richard Saks might be trampled, the porter pulled him up to lean against the wall. As he did, Tom spotted the bloody knife.

"Have you got a hankie?" he asked the porter.

The old man nodded, and reached into his pocket. Tom knelt down, studying the strong blade and handle of the hunting knife, then wrapped it carefully in the hankie. He looked up, and saw the face of Richard Saks close by, the sour smell of alcohol on his breath.

"No," Richard Saks said, his eyes desperate. "No, little chum, I didn't do it."

"Liar!" The short, fat man raised his hand, ready to hit Richard Saks again. "I'll make you tell the truth!"

Tom leaned toward Richard Saks, trying to shield him from a blow, but someone grabbed the threatening hand. Tom looked up and saw a big man in a conductor's uniform.

"All right," the conductor said, "what's going on?"

Everyone answered at once, but nothing made sense to the conductor until Tom unwrapped the hankie to display the bloody knife. Then the man went into action, clearing the corridor of spectators before escorting Richard Saks to Bedroom E, which was empty. The porter was ordered inside to guard Richard Saks, then the door was locked and the conductor turned to Tom and the other witnesses.

"Please return to your beds," he said. "I'll radio ahead to the next town, and have the police meet the train. I'm sure they'll want to speak to you all."

It seemed forever to the next town. Tom lay on his bed, unable to forget the first sight of Richard Saks holding the bloody knife, and at last saw a small bubble of light appear ahead in the darkness. Slowly it grew, until Tom could make out streetlights and the colours of neon signs.

The train pulled into the town, whistle blowing and bell clanging as if it wanted to tell everyone of the horrors which had occurred. Tom sat up, and was putting on his shoes when he saw a small station appear. Half the town must have been on the platform, staring, and he saw other people running toward the station as the train ground to a halt.

A police car was parked beside the station, its lights flashing. A Mountie got out and walked to the train; a few seconds later, Tom heard him talking to the conductor as they passed in the corridor. Then all was silence, and Tom turned back to the window.

As time passed the crowd grew larger, gathering in excited clusters under the bare lightbulbs which lit the platform. A man wearing a short-sleeved shirt, hands in the pockets of his trousers, looked up at Tom and said something.

"What?" Tom said, unable to hear through the glass.

The man cupped his hands around his mouth. This time, his words squeezed through the window. "What happened?"

Tom looked down at the hunting knife in his hands. Unable to resist the temptation, he removed it from the hankie and held it up, as if ready to stab someone. The man's eyes bulged, then he shouted something and pointed at Tom. Excitement jumped like electricity through the crowd, and everyone pushed toward Tom's window, fighting for a view of the bloody knife.

Feeling embarrassed and stupid, Tom lowered the knife and pulled down his blind. Now he'd botched it! Some detective, not only showing off to a crowd of strangers, but getting his fingerprints on valuable evidence in the process. Hot with shame, Tom rolled up the knife in the hankie.

A hand was fumbling with Tom's curtains. His heart leaped in terror, but it was only the conductor, who looked in and said: "Would you come with me, please?"

The man led the way to the dome car, where the other witnesses to the tragedy sat at the small restaurant tables. Everyone wore dressing-gowns except the porter.

The Mountie sat at a table, a notebook in his hand. He was very young, with bright blue eyes and blond hair cut short. "Is this the final witness?" he asked the conductor.

"Yes."

The Mountie looked at Tom. "May I have your name?"

"Tom Austen." Trying not to blush, Tom held out the knife. "I'm afraid this may have my fingerprints on it."

"Is that the knife Richard Saks used?"

"I don't know if he actually used it, but when I came into the corridor he was holding it in his hands, then dropped it."

The short, fat man leaned forward in his seat. "He used it all right!" he said angrily. "He murdered his own wife."

"Can you prove it?" Tom asked.

"Of course I can. We all heard them fighting in the bar, and then Saks said he hated the sight of his wife."

"But that's not proof!" Tom said.

"It is to me."

"And to me," the cookie-woman said, drawing her blue dressing-gown tighter around her body.

"Don't forget they were fighting last night in their compartment."

"You weren't there," Tom said. "You don't know what happened."

"But I was," the porter said, his eyes jumping nervously between Tom and the conductor.

"So was I," Mrs. Ruggles said. She wore a woolly dressing-gown over a long, white nightdress, and tears had stained her cheeks. "It sounded like a very angry fight."

"Yes, I suppose it was," Tom said quietly. He hated to think of Richard Saks being a murderer, but all the evidence was against the man. Even worse, Tom suddenly remembered their conversation at the breakfast table. It made things blacker for Richard Saks, but Tom couldn't keep evidence from the police. "There's something else," he said miserably.

"What's that?" the Mountie asked.

"My friend and I had breakfast with Mr. Saks and his wife. She said she wanted to be free again in order to return to Hollywood, and Mr. Saks looked very upset."

The short, fat man slapped his hand against the table. "There's your motive!" he shouted. "He knew he was losing his wife, so he killed her."

"Perhaps," the Mountie said. He looked down at his notebook. "Let me take a moment to reconstruct events."

Despite feeling sorry for Richard Saks, Tom was thrilled to be this close to a murder investigation. He watched the Mountie with fascination as he read from his notes:

"Saks and his wife were heard fighting in their compartment. Yesterday morning, at breakfast, his wife expressed an interest in leaving him. In the evening, they were heard quarrelling in the bar, and she returned alone to her compartment." The Mountie paused, and looked around. "Correct so far?"

Several heads nodded.

"At midnight Richard Saks left the bar, very drunk, and returned to his compartment." The Mountie looked over at the old lady. "Mrs. Ruggles was awakened by the sound of a violent struggle, then heard Catherine Saks cry out in terror. She raised the alarm, and young Tom Austen was the first to come to her aid."

Tom tried to look modest.

"Tom Austen saw Richard Saks holding a bloody knife, which he then dropped. Seconds later the man was overpowered by the porter, and Catherine Saks was discovered in her bedroom, dead from a number of savage stab wounds."

Tom shivered, glad now that he hadn't seen the inside of Bedroom C. How horrible, to think of that beautiful woman lying in a pool of blood.

"In fairness to Richard Saks," the Mountie went on, "he does deny that he murdered his wife. He says he found her dead, picked up the knife and went into the corridor to seek help. However, he admits to being drunk at the time, and says his memory of events is very foggy."

Tom remembered Richard Saks sitting in the bar, looking down at his drink. If only he had gone to bed when Tom had stopped to say good night. Suddenly, and unhappily, Tom remembered more evidence.

"Excuse me, sir," he said, "but I just thought of something. This evening, when I wished Richard Saks a good night, he looked unhappy and said, 'It won't be for me.' "

The short, fat man looked at the Mountie. "Well?" he demanded, as if addressing an infant. "Now are you going to take my advice, and charge Saks with murder?"

The Mountie gave the man a dirty look, and it was clear who he'd like to put behind bars. "Yes, I'm going to arrest Richard Saks," he said, "on suspicion of murder."

"That's better." The man looked around. "We're all taxpayers, so it's our duty to be sure the police operate efficiently."

The cookie-woman nodded, and stood up. "May we go now?" she asked the Mountie. "You've kept us awake half the night."

"Yes, you may go."

As the people filed out, Tom saw the Mountie shake his head in disgust. No wonder, when he was under attack as he tried to get the facts on a murder. Deeply upset by the events of the night, Tom walked back to his berth. Dietmar's face appeared between his curtains.

"Is Catherine Saks really dead?" he asked. Tom nodded.

"I hope that guy gets strung up."

"Who?"

"Her husband."

"How do you know he murdered her?"

"It's obvious. He's just like the killers you see on TV."

"Very clever, Dietmar."

Tom climbed into his berth and peeked out the

blind at the crowd. He felt like getting out of the train for some fresh air, but what if he was recognized as the boy with the knife?

A disguise would help. Tom got out of his berth and dug in his suitcase for a pair of sunglasses and his blazer. Putting them on, he walked to the far end of the restaurant car so that he could slip quietly out of the train. The door was open, and Tom hurried down the steps.

Every face was turned toward the sleeping-car where Catherine Saks lay dead, and no one noticed Tom leave the train. Spotting a boy leaning against his bike near the station, Tom walked over.

"Hi," he said, "what's going on?"

"There's been a murder!" the boy answered, his voice thrilled.

"What happened?"

"See that car?" the boy said, pointing to Tom's sleeping-car.

"Yeah."

"Some kid stabbed his mother to death. They locked him in a bedroom until the train reached here, but he escaped and cut up some people who tried to grab him."

Tom stared at the boy, unable to believe his ears.

"You see that window? That's where Hank Sayer saw the kid, waving a big carving knife dripping blood, his eyes rolling around like a madman. Then someone grabbed the kid, but he fought free and now he's hiding somewhere in the train."

The boy stopped talking, breathless with excitement.

"Why don't you go home?" Tom asked. "The kid might sneak off the train, and stab you with his knife."

The boy laughed. "I wouldn't miss this for the world."

"Well, see you around."

"Sure thing."

Tom stuck his hands in the pockets of his blazer and walked along the platform. There was a stir in the crowd, and he saw two men push past carrying a stretcher. Voices buzzed, and people stood on tiptoe to watch as the men climbed into the train. A few minutes later, someone close to the train cried out, "Here they come!"

The men with the stretcher appeared, struggling to get down the steps with their burden. The crowd fell silent, staring at the grey blanket that covered the body of Catherine Saks. Some of the men took off their hats, and Tom saw a woman touch a hankie to her eyes. As the stretcher was carried toward a waiting ambulance, the only sound was the hiss of steam from the train.

All eyes stared at the ambulance as the stretcher was loaded inside, but Tom happened to glance toward the train and saw the Mountie leading Richard Saks down the steps of the sleeping-car.

The two men cut around the back of the crowd and headed for the Mountie's car. Anxious to see Richard Saks a final time, Tom ran quickly to the car and reached it as the Mountie was opening the door.

"Good luck," Tom said to Richard Saks.

The man hardly seemed to recognize Tom, but he managed a small smile before sitting down wearily in the car. The Mountie got in, started the engine and drove quickly away, the wheels throwing dust up into the still, night air. Tom turned and walked slowly back to the train, unable to forget the sadness he had seen in the eyes of Richard Saks.

6

The next morning the sun was shining. Tom woke slowly, remembering the murder with a painful lurch of his heart. Poor Richard Saks.

He opened his eyes and glanced out the window. A huge mountain rose up into the sky, massive in the sunshine. He sat up wondering where the prairie had gone, then remembered the train was now in the Rocky Mountains.

The mountain was a giant slab of rock, its head reaching up among puffy clouds. Green trees clung to its side, and spread across the valley through which *The Canadian* was passing.

Tom pulled on his clothes while he enjoyed the

view. The train struggled up a steep climb, then made its way carefully along a narrow passage cut into the face of a cliff. Looking down into the valley, Tom saw an emerald-green lake, absolutely still except for a V of water spreading out behind a red canoe.

Tom didn't want to give up the view for even a minute, but he was terribly hungry. Opening his curtains, he debated whether to awaken Dietmar, then decided to go alone to the dining-car.

Only a few passengers were up this early, but one of them was the old lady, Mrs. Ruggles, wearing a black dress with puffy sleeves, and her shawl. Smiling, she beckoned Tom to her table.

"Good morning," he said, sitting down.

"Isn't it lovely?" Mrs. Ruggles said, pointing at the thick green forest in the valley below.

"It certainly is," Tom said, then glanced at his watch. " The Mountie's investigation sure put the train far behind schedule."

"Yes," Mrs. Ruggles said, "but it does give us extra time to enjoy the scenery."

Tom wrote out an order for Rice Krispies with cream, toast and milk, then stared out the window. "I wish Richard Saks could be looking at these mountains, instead of rotting in a cell."

"Yes, the poor man." Mrs. Ruggles shivered. "Please, let's not talk about it. Where do you live?"

"Winnipeg. My Dad is on the police force there."

"I live in Winnipeg, too. You must come for a visit, and we'll have some tea."

"Didn't you board the train in Brandon?"

"I was there visiting friends. Now I'm going to see my grandchildren at the coast," Mrs. Ruggles said and smiled happily. "I can't wait to see them again."

Tom poured cream into his bowl of Rice Krispies and picked up his spoon, which flashed silver in the sunshine. "Do you have a picture of them?"

"Who?"

"Your grandchildren."

"No, I'm afraid I don't."

"That's strange," Tom said, smiling. "My grand-parents have fifty million pictures of me and my sister." Chewing his cereal, he looked up high to the top of a mountain, where the frozen whiteness of a glacier stood out against the rock. "Last week I dropped my alarm clock in the river, and it's still running."

"That's amazing!" Mrs. Ruggles said.

"Well, it takes a lot to stop a river running."

The old lady laughed. "Have you heard the Little Moron jokes?"

"No," Tom lied. "Would you tell me some?"

"All right," Mrs. Ruggles said, beaming happily. "Why did the Little Moron take oats to bed?"

"I give up."

"He wanted to feed his nightmare."

Tom laughed. "That's great."

"Why did the Little Moron jump off the Empire State Building?" Silence, while Tom pretended to think. "He wanted to try his new spring coat."

Smiling, Tom spread marmalade on his toast, then said, "Adam and Eve and Pinch-me went down to the river to swim. Adam and Eve were drowned, so who was saved?"

"Pinch-me."

"Okay," Tom said, reaching over and lightly pinching the old lady's arm.

"Oh, you devil!" Mrs. Ruggles said, laughing. She finished her tea, then reached for her cane and stood up. "It's been lovely chatting with you, Tom. Perhaps you'd like to come to my compartment for a visit later, and we'll have some fudge and tell jokes."

"Great," Tom said. "I'll see you after."

The old lady hobbled away leaning heavily on her cane. When she was gone Tom looked down into the valley, where tiny cars crawled along a highway. Then, everything went black.

Lights came on in the dining-car, and Tom realized

the train had entered a tunnel. Leaning close to the window, he saw the train's lights bouncing off the jagged rocks of the tunnel wall. A few minutes later sunshine burst on to Tom's face, making his eyes sting. Finishing his toast, he stood up and walked back through the train.

Reaching his car, Tom pushed open the door and saw a little boy in a baseball cap looking in the door of a roomette, where the old porter was making up the bed. Turning toward Tom, the little boy pulled out a water pistol.

"Reach!" he said.

Smiling, Tom held up his hands. The boy fired, soaking Tom's shirt, then turned and ran.

The porter laughed. "That brat has been bugging me for an hour. I'd like to amputate his head."

Tom smiled politely, unpleasantly reminded of the knife that had been used on Catherine Saks. "Any more news about the murder?" he asked.

"Nope, nothing more," the old man said, his words making the curious whistling sound in the gap between his front teeth. "I guess that fella will spend his life in prison."

Tom glanced along the corridor, and saw the little boy sneaking toward him with the water pistol.

Caught, the boy fired quickly and retreated. Wiping water off his face, Tom wondered how someone could look so innocent yet be such a menace.

Finished with his duties in the roomette, the porter lit a cigarette. "I was plenty nervous giving evidence last night," he said.

"Why?"

"Man, at night I'm supposed to sit on a little chair in the corridor, in case people ring for something. If I'd been at my post last night, I would have heard the fight and prevented the murder."

"Where were you?"

"Sneaking a nap in Bedroom E." The old man puffed on his cigarette, then shook his head. "If that conductor finds out, I'll be fired."

"Well, I won't tell him," Tom said. He turned to walk away, then stopped, curious. "Was it pretty awful last night, in that woman's bedroom?"

"Man, there was blood everywhere. And vomit, all over the corpse."

"Vomit?" Tom said, surprised. "I thought she was stabbed to death."

"That's right. I guess that fella was so upset, he got sick."

Tom looked carefully at the porter. "Can you

remember if there was a smell in the bedroom?"

"Sure, it was awful, all that vomit and blood."

"But, was there an almond smell?"

The porter stared at Tom in surprise. "Man, how did you know? Did you sneak into that bedroom last night?"

Suddenly excited, but not wanting it to show, Tom shrugged his shoulders. "Nope, I wasn't there. Listen, are you sure?"

"Sure as the day I was born. I spent half the night trying to get that smell out of there."

Unable to contain his excitement, Tom grinned at the porter. "Thanks a million!" he said.

Tom turned and hurried through the car. Dietmar was crawling out of the upper berth, a big yawn on his face.

"Dietmar!" Tom said. "Have I got news for you!"

"The sky is falling," Dietmar said sarcastically. "Richard Saks is . . ." Tom said, then faltered. The cookie-woman was staring at him, her ears flapping. Boy, he'd almost botched it again!

"Come on," Tom said to Dietmar, dragging him toward the washroom.

"I want my breakfast," Dietmar protested.

"Later, later." Tom opened the washroom door,

hauled Dietmar inside and locked the door. Then he stepped to the sink and turned on the hot and cold taps.

"I'm old enough to wash myself," Dietmar said.

"That's not what the water's for," Tom whispered. "If the washroom is bugged, the running water will cover our words."

Dietmar laughed. "You're the one that's bugged, Austen."

"Listen," Tom said, eyes wide with excitement. "I just found out that Richard Saks is not the murderer!"

"Who is, the cookie-woman?"

"She might be. Everyone is a suspect."

"Why?"

"Listen to this," Tom said, dropping his voice lower. "Catherine Saks was poisoned with cyanide!"

"Says who?"

"Says me. The porter told me there was vomit on her body, and an almond smell in the bedroom."

"So what?"

"That smell, and the fact she vomited before dying, means cyanide poisoning."

"How do you know?" Dietmar asked, sounding less sarcastic.

"I read it in a detective book."

"You and your books," Dietmar said, shaking his head. "I think you're crazy. Richard Saks murdered his wife, and now he's in prison. Anyway, I heard she was stabbed to death."

"Sure, she was stabbed," Tom said, "but only after she was dead. That was to disguise the fact that she had been poisoned."

"Then Richard Saks must have given her cyanide."

"But why would he use both poison and a knife? No, someone else poisoned Catherine Saks and then stabbed the dead body to make it look like Richard Saks had murdered his wife in a drunken rage."

"Who?"

"I don't know," Tom admitted, "but I suspect everyone. For example, the cookie-woman might have given Catherine Saks a chocolate-chip-with-cyanide cookie."

Dietmar laughed, and opened the washroom door. "I'm going for my breakfast," he said, then thought of something and closed the door. "I may have a lead for you," he whispered.

"What's that?" Tom asked, excited.

"Last night I was standing beside a berth, Lower Two in Car 165, and I heard someone muttering in his sleep about bloody knives and dead bodies."

"Hold it!" Tom said, reaching into his pocket for the notebook he always carried. "Let me write that down."

Dietmar repeated the information, then left for his breakfast. Tom hesitated, uncertain how to follow up the lead, then decided to reconnoitre the car and see who occupied the berth. Leaving the washroom, he suddenly remembered he was already in Car 165. Not only that, Lower Two was his own berth!

Swearing he'd get even with Dietmar, Tom went to his seat and began to make notes on the murder. First, he made a sketch of Car 165, with a chart indicating who occupied the various berths and bedrooms. Then he noted what he'd seen and heard last night, and the evidence given to the Mountie. Finally, he recorded his suspicion that Catherine Saks had been poisoned.

Tom leaned back in his seat, staring at the notebook. Somewhere, in that tangle of evidence, were the clues which pointed to the real killer. He must work it out before the train reached Vancouver!

"Hi, mister."

Tom looked up from his notebook and saw the little boy in the baseball cap.

"I'm sorry I shot you, mister." The little boy took

a package of gum from his pocket. "If you forgive me, I'll give you a piece of gum."

"Sure, kid, I forgive you." Tom only chewed Dubble Bubble, but he thought he should make the boy feel better. "Okay, give me some."

Smiling happily, the little boy held out his hand. Tom reached for a stick of gum, and was pulling it out of the package when there was a buzzing sound, and a flash of pain shot up his arm.

"Ow!" Tom yelled, dropping the gum.

The little boy laughed with joy, grabbed the booby-trapped gum from the floor and ran quickly away. Across the aisle, the cookie-woman tried to smother a laugh.

His face red with embarrassment, Tom did his best to smile at the woman. "That kid," he said. "I'd like to amputate his head."

"Don't you dare!" the woman said, shocked.

"Okay, maybe just one foot. Then I can catch him when he tries to run away."

The woman gave Tom a dirty look, then sniffed and turned her head. If she was looking for the killer, Tom realized, he would be the number one suspect.

Enough wasting time. Tom turned back to his notebook, studying the evidence, searching for a lead.

As he worked, Dietmar returned and slumped down in his seat, a toothpick in his mouth.

"The butler did it," he said, grinning.

"Drop on your head," Tom muttered, busy with his pen.

"Have you got a magnifying glass?"

"What for?"

"I can't wait to see you crawling around the floor, searching for clues like Sherlock Holmes."

"Funny, funny." Tom would never admit it to Dietmar, but he had already tried to picture how Sherlock Holmes would investigate this case. Probably he really would start by crawling around for clues. "Hey," Tom said, "I've got an idea!"

"Kill it before it grows."

Tom leaned toward Dietmar. "I'm going to get into Bedroom C, and search for clues," he whispered.

"How?"

"Maybe the door is unlocked." Tom stood up. "Coming?"

"I don't know," Dietmar said, trying to sound bored. "Okay, I guess so."

Tom led the way to Bedroom C. He glanced up and down the corridor, then tried the door, but it was locked. "Rats!" he said. "What a bad break."

"Why don't you ask the porter to open it?"

"Good thinking, Dietmar. Maybe I'll hire you as my assistant."

The porter was busy in Bedroom A, but Tom noticed there was no sign of its occupant, the man with the attaché case. He wondered briefly why he hadn't seen the man around lately, then looked at the porter.

"Hi," he said, "how's it going?"

"Okay, man. I hear you got zapped by the brat."

"What happened?" Dietmar asked.

"Nothing," Tom said, waving his hand. "Listen, sir, could you do me a favour?"

"What's that?"

"Let me see inside Bedroom C."

The porter laughed. "Man, you are some blood-thirsty kid."

Wanting to hide his real reason for seeing the bedroom, Tom bared his teeth like Dracula. "Blooooood, blooooood," he hissed, "give me blooooood."

Chuckling, the porter reached into his pocket for a key ring. "Okay, but let's make it fast."

"Great!" Tom said.

The porter led the way to Bedroom C. As he turned the key, Tom trembled, afraid of what he might see inside. But the porter had worked hard to clean up the bedroom, and the sun beamed happily through the window.

"There's nothing to see," Dietmar said, disappointed. Tom opened the door to the toilet and looked inside. Nothing. He checked the cabinet over the sink, but the porter had done his work well. His heart sinking, Tom glanced around the carpet, then walked to the window, hoping for fingerprints.

"I gotta get back to work," the porter said.

"Okay," Tom said unhappily. Turning from the window, he noticed a small ashtray mounted in the wall. Inside was a cigarette butt.

"Here's something you missed," Tom said.

"What?" The porter walked to Tom's side, and laughed. "A butt! Man, I'm glad you're not president of this railway or I'd be fired. Here, I'll get that."

"No, let me," Tom said, reaching quickly for the butt. He slipped it in his pocket, and smiled at the porter. "Well, thanks a lot, man."

The porter laughed. "See you later."

The cookie-woman looked up suspiciously when they returned to their seats, so Tom dragged Dietmar on to the washroom. Locking the door, and turning on the taps, he took the cigarette butt out of his pocket.

"This could be a lead," he said hopefully.

"No," Dietmar said, "it's a butt."

Tom examined the butt closely, trying to make out the brand name. "I think it says Players," he said, "but this lipstick stain covers most of the name."

"What brand did Catherine Saks smoke at breakfast?"

"I don't know," Tom said, ashamed of his ability as a detective. Every book told him to concentrate on being observant, and now he'd failed. He strained his memory of the breakfast table, but all he could recall was how elegant the long cigarette holder had made Catherine Saks look. "Well," he sighed, "maybe it's nothing."

Returning with Dietmar to their seats, Tom pulled out his suitcase and found one of the envelopes his mother had given him for writing home. He put the cigarette butt inside, then wrote on the envelope the date, time of day, and his initials. Putting it in his pocket, he picked up the notebook.

"Back to square one," he said mournfully.

"I told you," Dietmar said, putting his feet on Tom's seat, "the butler did it."

Before long, Dietmar was asleep. Tom laboured over his notebook, too busy to look out at the beauty of the mountains. A waiter had just walked through the car announcing lunch, and Dietmar was snoring noisily, when Tom snapped his fingers and looked up, delighted.

"Hey," he said to himself, "I think I've got it!"

7

Tom grabbed Dietmar's arm. "Quick," he said, "wake up!"

Dietmar's eyes flew open. "What?" he shouted. "Murder? Murder?"

"No, no," Tom said, holding up his notebook. "I've figured it out!"

Across the aisle the cookie-woman snapped shut a book she'd been reading. "You boys stop making all that noise, or I'll ring for the porter."

"Yes, ma'am!" Tom said, grinning. Pulling Dietmar out of his seat, he headed for the washroom.

"That woman must think we're crazy," Dietmar said, "always going to the washroom together."

"Nuts to her," Tom said, so excited he forgot to turn on the taps. "I know who the killer is."

"Who?"

"The man with the attaché case!"

"Why?"

"It's all in here," Tom said, slapping his notebook. "When we were playing bingo, that man called Richard Saks a drunk, and said he was no good."

"So what?"

"I thought it was strange he knew Richard Saks by name, but he pretended he'd seen it in the newspaper." Tom looked closely at Dietmar. "If he'd only heard of Richard Saks from the newspaper, why would he say 'the man is no good'?"

"Yeah, that's weird. But why kill Catherine Saks?"

"I'm coming to that." Tom opened the notebook and checked his information. "When I asked him what was in his attaché case, he said it was paper worth a million dollars. There's the motive."

"I don't get it."

"Blackmail!" Tom waited for a reaction, but Dietmar only stared. "Haven't you read anything by Agatha Christie?"

"Nope."

"You illiterate," Tom said, shaking his head. "Well,

in her detective books you always have to watch for a blackmail angle. When I remembered that, my case fell together."

"I still don't get it."

"I think Catherine Saks did something bad in Hollywood. That man found out, and has the details on the paper in his attaché case, which is why he won't let it out of his sight. He threatened to reveal the truth, so Richard Saks paid blackmail. But the man kept asking for more and more money, until finally Richard Saks threatened to go to the police."

"Okay so far."

"The night we played bingo, that man followed Catherine Saks to her bedroom and poisoned her. Then he stabbed her to make it look like Richard Saks was the murderer. That way, no one will believe Richard Saks if he ever claims he was being black-mailed."

"Well," Dietmar said, "it's pretty complicated, but it all adds up. Are you going to tell the conductor?"

"Yes, but first I want to get some additional proof. I'm going to find that man and ask a few innocent questions, then try to get a look inside his attaché case. If I could see those blackmail papers, it would really seal my case."

Dietmar swallowed nervously. "You'd better be careful," he said. "If he suspects anything, he'll murder you, too."

Tom smiled as bravely as possible. "Don't worry, I won't accept any poisoned food."

The washroom door creaked as Tom opened it. He hadn't noticed the creak before, but now his nerves were on edge. He looked up and down the train, then hurried back to his seat, heart thumping. It was one thing to read the Hardy Boys stories, but something else to be actually chasing a killer.

"What next?" Dietmar whispered.

"I'm going to find that man," Tom answered. "Wish me luck."

"Okay, but be careful."

Tom put the notebook in his pocket and walked toward the bedroom corridor. At the far end, the porter sat on a folding seat, a cigarette smouldering in his fingers. Seeing Tom, the man smiled.

"Hiya, Dracula," he said. "Going to the bar for a bottle of blood?"

Tom smiled. "Maybe later. Right now, I'm going to visit that man in Bedroom A."

"You can't do that."

"Why not?"

"He's gone to the dining-car for lunch."

"Oh," Tom said, hesitating. "Well, I'm kind of hungry myself. Think I'll go have a steak."

"Hey, a moneybags. I'll expect a giant tip when we reach Vancouver."

Heading for the dining-car, Tom stopped to check his finances. His parents had only given him money to buy a cheeseburger for lunch, but he had to follow the man. Well, he could spend his dinner money now and starve tonight.

In the dining-car, Tom saw Mrs. Ruggles sitting alone with a pot of tea. She smiled happily and beckoned to him, but at the same moment he spotted the man with the attaché case, alone at another table.

Slowly, Tom walked over to Mrs. Ruggles. "Hi," he said, his mind searching rapidly for excuses.

"Sit down, please," Mrs. Ruggles said. "How wonderful of you to come, just when I was feeling lonely."

"I'd like to sit with you, but I can't."

"Oh," Mrs. Ruggles said, unable to hide her disappointment. "Aren't you having lunch?"

"Yes, but . . ." Tom's face was beginning to burn. "I, uh, promised to have lunch with someone else."

"Oh." Obviously Mrs. Ruggles knew Tom was lying, but she smiled. "Have fun, then, and perhaps I'll see you later."

"Sure," Tom said miserably. He walked away, feeling terrible about hurting the old lady's feelings, but a detective had to be ruthless.

The man with the attaché case was reading a letter. As Tom approached he quickly put it away and pretended to be staring out the window.

"Hi," Tom said, sitting down at the man's table, "mind if I join you?"

The man looked at Tom with a thin smile. "I don't seem to have much choice."

Tom held out his hand. "My name is Tom Austen."

"You can call me Mr. Faith." The man's handshake was quick, and limp. "Or Mr. Hope, or Mr. Charity."

Aliases? Tom's mind prickled with suspicion as he studied the man's grey hair, the dry skin of his narrow face, his tiny brown eyes. Certainly the face of a killer, but that was no proof. Get to work, Austen, he told himself.

"Going far?"

Again, the thin smile. "I thought so, when I was a young man. But life's plans often go astray."

"No, I mean on this train."

"Oh, I see." Mr. Faith looked out the window at the passing forest, and his attention seemed to drift. "This is the most important journey of my life," he said at last.

Tom waited for more, but obviously the man didn't intend to give a direct answer. Not wanting to arouse his suspicions, Tom pretended to lose interest and picked up the menu. The cheapest item was a Spanish omelette, which sounded horrible, but he had to order something.

"Ah yes," Mr. Faith sighed, "I have dreamed my dreams, and reached for the stars."

Was this guy nuts? Perhaps committing that gruesome murder had pushed him over the brink into insanity. Tom looked around the dining-car to see who could help in an emergency, but Mrs. Ruggles was gone and the only other passenger he recognized was the short, fat man, who seemed half asleep in the sunshine.

As he waited for the Spanish omelette to arrive, Tom considered and rejected various approaches, finally deciding to attack directly. Summoning courage, he looked at Mr. Faith.

"Do you know Richard Saks?"

Startled, the man turned from the window. "What?"

"Is Richard Saks a friend of yours?"

Mr. Faith laughed bitterly. "Certainly not," he said. "I hate him."

Tom almost gasped, he was so surprised that his theory was right. As he stared at Mr. Faith, a waiter arrived with a steaming yellow mass on a plate.

"Your omelette, sir," the waiter said, depositing the plate on the tablecloth.

"Thanks," Tom said weakly. He cut into the omelette, but was sickened to discover it full of green things.

Mr. Faith smiled unpleasantly at Tom. *"Bon appétit,"* he said, lifting his water glass in a mock toast.

Bon appétit? The same curious words the dining-car steward had spoken to Tom at breakfast. Perhaps the two men were partners in crime, and the steward had provided the poisoned food used to kill Catherine Saks. His hands trembling, Tom looked down at the omelette, thankful he hadn't yet taken a bite.

"Not hungry?" Mr. Faith asked. Tom shook his head.

"Then why waste money ordering that omelette?" Mr. Faith said, wrinkling his small mouth disapprovingly. "If you were my son, I'd make you eat it."

Tom shivered, pitying any kid who had Mr. Faith for a father. Glancing out the window, he saw the diesel slowing as it approached a tunnel. Afraid the man might try something while the train was in the tunnel, Tom pushed back his chair and got ready to run.

"Not another tunnel," Mr. Faith said as the train entered the darkness and the dining-car lights came on. "This is ridiculous."

The train continued to slow down until it was only creeping, increasing Tom's nervousness. For a horrible moment he thought even the engineer was part of the plot, then realized that was silly. Still, he greeted the return of sunshine with relief.

"Eat your omelette before it gets cold," Mr. Faith said. "You mustn't waste it."

Tom was caught. He couldn't eat the poisoned omelette, but he must not make the man suspicious. Slowly, he picked up his knife and fork, then put them down and reached for his water glass.

"Do you know any jokes?" Tom said, hoping to distract the man's attention from the uneaten omelette.

"This rail service is a joke," Mr. Faith said, looking out the window as the train crept into another tunnel. When the lights came on, he raised his hand and snapped his fingers. "Come here, my good man," he called.

Tom turned, and saw a conductor about to sit down for a meal at the crew table. Hearing Mr. Faith call, the man walked down the car.

"Yes, sir?" he said.

"Why is this train moving so slowly?"

"Repair work in the tunnels, sir. There's a risk of falling rock."

"What a nuisance." Mr. Faith pulled back his cuff and tapped the face of his watch. "We're already late because of that wretched murder, and now more delays. I must get to Vancouver as soon as possible."

"Yes, sir," the conductor said, touching his cap. "I'll ask the engineer to pedal faster."

"None of your cheek," Mr. Faith said, his dull skin turning red. "I can get you fired."

"Yes, sir. In the meantime, may I eat my lunch?"

Mr. Faith watched the conductor walk away, then looked at Tom's plate. "Ah, I see you've eaten your omelette."

"Yes, it was delicious."

"That's better," Mr. Faith said, the tense lines on his face relaxing. "I've never had much money, so I hate to see anything wasted."

Tom's lap was becoming very warm. He glanced down at the omelette, which lay in the middle of a napkin on his lap, where he had shoved it during Mr. Faith's argument with the conductor. Keeping his eyes on the man, Tom carefully folded the linen napkin around the omelette, and dropped it on the floor.

That danger past, Tom returned to the attack. "Why do you hate Richard Saks?" he asked, watching for Mr. Faith's reaction.

"Oh, look," the man said, pointing out the window, "that's rather pretty."

Tom looked out at a stream which lay beside the tracks, its emerald waters shaded by trees along the bank. A fisherman wearing hip-waders stood in the stream, flicking his line toward a pool of deep, cold water.

"I needed some money," Mr. Faith said, "so I went to the bank where Richard Saks was manager. He turned me down."

"Why?"

"He said I was a poor risk," Mr. Faith said bitterly. "He said I should get a job if I needed money."

"Don't you have one?"

"Not a typical job, like driving a bus or pulling teeth." Mr. Faith paused, and swallowed some water. "I work on my own, and only get money from time to time. That's why I needed the loan."

The evidence was piling up. Everything Mr. Faith was saying showed that he was a blackmailer with a strong motive for revenge against Richard Saks. All that remained was somehow to get a look inside the attaché case.

"Richard Saks is a scoundrel," Mr. Faith said. "Because of him, an innocent person went to prison."

"What happened?"

"A few years ago, some money was embezzled from his bank, which means it was stolen by someone who worked there. The police suspected Richard Saks, but at his trial evidence turned up which led to the conviction of a cashier. She went to prison, and Richard Saks was set free, but a lot of people think he framed the cashier."

"Was there any proof?"

"No, but that's just the sort of double-cross that he'd do." The tension had returned to Mr. Faith's face, pinching the skin round his eyes and mouth. "You can never trust a man with a beautiful wife."

"Well," Tom said quietly, "he doesn't have her any more."

"That's true," the man said, cheering up. "And I can't say I'm sorry."

Someone was approaching. Tom looked up, and saw the conductor, cap in hand. "Excuse me, sir," he said to Mr. Faith, "but you'll want to know we'll be stopping for fifteen minutes at the town we're approaching. I regret the inconvenience, but the diesel has difficulty working unless given fuel."

"I know how diesels work," Mr. Faith snapped.

"Anyway, I'll be happy to get off for a walk, away from smart-alec conductors."

"I'll come with you," Tom said, standing up.

"I'd rather go alone." Mr. Faith wiped his mouth delicately with his napkin, then took the attaché case from his lap and stood up. "Goodbye, young man."

Mr. Faith put some change on the table and walked away, the silver chain clinking at his wrist. Quickly, Tom counted out enough money to pay for the omelette, then rushed after Mr. Faith.

He found him standing in the vestibule between the dining-car and the next sleeping-car, waiting for the train to stop. The rattle and bang of the wheels made speaking difficult, so Tom just smiled at Mr. Faith and looked out the window.

The train pulled to a stop beside a little station made of red bricks. The young porter, Dermot, opened the door and threw back the steel panel covering the steps, then descended to the platform.

"Fifteen-minute stop," he said, as Mr. Faith quickly left the train.

Tom caught up to Mr. Faith on the platform, and fell into step at his side. "Hi," he said brightly, "doesn't the mountain air smell good?"

No answer.

"Wow, look at those peaks," Tom said, pointing up at the frozen snow sparkling in the clean air. "Wouldn't you love to climb up there?"

Mr. Faith made a sudden left turn off the platform, cut between two cars in the station parking lot and hurried away. Tom was caught flat-footed, but he ran after the man and reached his side as he started along a street of ancient wooden houses.

"Why are you going to Vancouver?" Tom asked.

Mr. Faith stopped walking, and stared down at Tom. There was a long pause, the only sound the rusty creaking of a swing in a front yard, then Mr. Faith took a coin from his pocket.

"Why don't you go buy a Coke?" he said, holding out the money.

"Thanks, but there are no shops here."

Mr. Faith turned impatiently to look up and down the street. "There!" he said triumphantly, pointing toward an old building with a flickering neon sign reading CAFÉ.

"It looks awful," Tom said, staring at the café. "I'm nervous to go there alone."

"Come on," Mr. Faith said, taking Tom by the arm. "I'll buy you a Coke, and then you can leave me in peace."

No chance of that, but Tom didn't say so. By sticking close to Mr. Faith, he was deliberately applying mental pressure which would eventually make the man crack. Then he would make a mistake, and Tom would get his final proof.

"What kind of papers do you have in your case?" he asked.

No answer from Mr. Faith, who seemed lost in thought. They passed a general store, its window displaying faded merchandise and a sleeping cat, and crossed the street to the café.

Mr. Faith opened a screen door and they stepped into a dim interior smelling of greasy food. Tom blinked, adjusting his eyes to the darkness, and saw a waitress wearing a stained uniform.

"Off the train?" she said. "What'll you have?"

"A Coke for this young man," Mr. Faith said, "and I'll have a coffee if it's hot, and made today."

The woman looked angrily at Mr. Faith and turned to open a small hatch leading to the kitchen. "One Coke, one coffee!" she hollered, then banged the hatch shut.

Mr. Faith sat down at the counter, putting the attaché case on his lap. As Tom sat down on a stool, Mr. Faith took a paper napkin from a dispenser and carefully wiped the counter.

"How about playing some music?" Tom said, pointing at a juke-box sagging in one corner of the café.

"Rock and roll," Mr. Faith muttered, then looked at the waitress. "Is there a washroom?"

"Through there," the woman said, pointing at a door.

Mr. Faith stood up, and went through the door. As he did, Tom caught a glimpse of a kitchen with a man in a cook's hat leaning over a stove. The door swung shut, and Tom did a couple of spins on his stool, then wandered over to look at the juke-box titles.

"Here's your Coke," the waitress called. "Better drink up fast, the train's leaving soon."

"Thanks," Tom said, smiling at her. His Coke waited in a tall glass on the counter, beside it a cup of coffee. But there was no sign of Mr. Faith.

Tom sat down, glancing nervously toward the kitchen door. Mr. Faith wouldn't have time for his coffee if he didn't hurry. He reached for the straws which stuck out of his glass, and used them to swirl the ice cubes while he wondered what was keeping the man.

"Drink up," the waitress said, "there's a good boy."

Where was Mr. Faith? The fifteen minutes were almost gone, and they still had to walk back to the station. Tom leaned forward to sip his Coke, but he felt too nervous about the train to drink. Pushing the glass away, he stood up.

"I'll be right back," he said to the woman.

She pointed at his drink and started to say something, but Tom was already through the door into the kitchen. A frying-pan spluttered on the stove, music came from a radio, and the cook was washing a big pot in a sink full of dirty water.

"Where's the washroom?" Tom asked the cook.

The man lifted a dripping hand out of the water and gestured toward a door. The way to it was cluttered with mops and brooms and cartons of food, but Tom got past them as quickly as possible and knocked on the door.

"Mr. Faith?" he called. "We've got to hurry, the train's leaving."

There was no answer, so Tom knocked again, louder this time. The seconds ticked away while Tom waited, until finally he could stand the suspense no longer. Reaching for the wooden handle, he pulled open the door. The washroom was empty.

8

Tom stared into the tiny room, then slammed the door and turned toward the cook.

"Where did he go?" he asked desperately.

The man didn't seem to hear. He pulled the plug in the sink, and watched as the grey water seeped slowly away.

"Please!" Tom said. "Where's the man gone?"

The cook reached for a towel hanging over the sink and began to dry his hands carefully. As he did, he made a nodding gesture with his head.

"Please," Tom repeated, "help me."

Again the man nodded, and this time Tom realized he was gesturing toward a door half hidden in a corner. He ran forward, hearing the last of the dish-water gurgle down the drain, and pulled open the door.

Sunshine struck his face. Blinded, Tom stumbled ahead, tears streaming from his eyes. As he began to make out the dim shapes of walls, a car, some trees, he heard the whistle of the train.

Wiping at the tears on his face, Tom began to run. The whistle came again, a warning to hurry. Slowly Tom's eyes adjusted to the sunlight, but they still stung as he dashed down the long dusty road toward the station.

Outside a house, two women were laughing together, unaware that the boy who rushed past was in such trouble. Not only tricked into missing the train, but tricked into botching his murder investigation! Unable to believe what had happened, Tom raced across the station parking lot as the whistle blew a final time.

The porter stood in the doorway of the sleeping-car, waving his arm. "Come on, man!" he yelled. "Move those feet!"

His breath red-hot in his throat, Tom stumbled across the platform and reached the sleeping-car. He saw the conductor wave toward the diesel, then the porter pulled him on to the steps of the car and the train lurched forward.

"Man," the porter said, "I had to make them hold the train."

"Thanks," Tom gasped, holding tight to the railing as he sucked air into his lungs.

"What happened?" the porter asked. "Mr. Faith said you were hanging around in a café, or something foolish like that."

"Is he on the train?"

"Sure is. Man, if you'd missed the train, I'd have lost my giant tip."

Tom smiled at the old man, feeling happy to know there was one person on the train he could trust. Where was Mr. Faith now? He had to find him, and demand an explanation for his trickery.

"Thanks again," Tom said, climbing the steps on shaky legs, glad to be safe inside the train instead of abandoned in the mountain town.

Inside the sleeping-car, Tom stopped at Bedroom A and knocked loudly. Now he really was afraid of Mr. Faith, but he was also angry, and that gave him a sense of courage. When there was no answer he knocked again, then looked up and down the corridor wonder- ing where the man was hiding.

The dome car was a possibility. As Tom started toward it, the short, fat man appeared ahead in the corridor. Tom kept walking, but the corridor was narrow and the man approached like a bull elephant apparently ready to flatten Tom if he didn't get out of the way. At the last second Tom saw an open bedroom door, jumped inside, and watched the man rumble past.

"Tom! You've come for your visit!"

Oh, no. What incredibly bad luck! Tom realized he had blundered into the bedroom occupied by Mrs. Ruggles. Remembering his promise to visit the old lady for jokes and fudge, and the way he had snubbed her in the dining-car, Tom closed his eyes miserably. He couldn't snub her again.

"Why did the Little Moron throw the clock out the window?"

Slowly Tom turned, trying to smile.

Mrs. Ruggles was sitting in a chair, a book on her lap. "Because he wanted to see time fly."

Tom managed to find a laugh, and pushed it through unhappy lips. This sort of thing never happened to the Hardy Boys, but he couldn't hurt the old lady's feelings again.

"Your turn for a joke," she said, pulling the shawl

tighter around her shoulders. "Close the door, and come join me."

Fighting the urge to run from the bedroom and continue his search for Mr. Faith, Tom reluctantly closed the door and turned to Mrs. Ruggles, who smiled in anticipation of his joke.

"Uh, let's see," Tom said, "uh, this kid went into a barber shop and the man asked if he wanted a haircut. 'No,' the kid said, 'I want them all cut.' "

Mrs. Ruggles didn't get it. She waited for the punch line, then smiled vaguely. "Very funny," she said, frowning in confusion.

Feeling sorry for the old lady's fading mind, and her loneliness, Tom resigned himself to spending half an hour with her before looking for Mr. Faith. He sat down facing Mrs. Ruggles and tried to think of a joke that she could understand.

"Here's a riddle," he said. "You know that a horse goes on four legs, right?"

"Yes."

"And a human goes on two legs."

Mrs. Ruggles nodded.

"So what goes on one leg?"

The old lady scrunched her forehead in concentration, and Tom could practically hear the wheels grinding inside her head, but it was no use. Smiling hopelessly, she looked at Tom for the answer.

"A boot!"

This time she understood, and laughed brightly. Reaching for her handbag, she took out a piece of fudge for Tom, then a cigarette package. "Do you mind if I smoke?" she asked.

Tom shook his head. Chewing the rich chocolate fudge, he looked around the bedroom. "What's that?" he asked, pointing at something that looked like a statue of a bald head, resting on the floor in a corner.

"Oh, that." Mrs. Ruggles lit her cigarette, and shook the match until it puffed out. "It's a wig stand."

"What's it for?"

"You put your wig on there at night, so it doesn't lose its shape overnight."

"Do you wear a wig?"

Mrs. Ruggles didn't answer, but instead looked confused and upset. Tom blushed, realizing he'd said the wrong thing. The poor old lady was probably as bald as a billiard ball, but naturally she didn't want anyone to know.

"Got another joke?" he asked, trying to change the subject.

"Let me think," Mrs. Ruggles said vaguely, puffing on her cigarette. "I used to know so many."

As the old lady strained her memory, the train rolled into a tunnel and its speed dropped to a walking pace. This tunnel was very long, and Tom smiled when he thought how annoyed the train's slow progress must be making Mr. Faith. But where was the man hiding?

"I must go soon," Tom said.

"Why?" Mrs. Ruggles asked, disappointed.

Tom smiled, embarrassed. "I'm working on a case," he said shyly.

"A case? What do you mean?"

Suddenly it all poured out of Tom. It felt good to talk to someone kind and sympathetic, and now he told the whole story of the cyanide and Mr. Faith and almost being left in the mountain town.

"And that's why I couldn't sit with you at lunch," he finished, thankful he could at last explain the snub.

During the story, Mrs. Ruggles had listened quietly, nodding her head, occasionally asking questions. Now she lit another cigarette and looked carefully at Tom. "Very, very clever," she said. "You really are a detective."

Tom grinned happily, unable to hide his pleasure. "Maybe you could help me!" he said. "We can find Mr. Faith, and then you ask him some questions about his attaché case. That might catch him off guard."

"That sounds like fun," Mrs. Ruggles said. She gave Tom more fudge, then stood up and walked to the washroom. "Excuse me a minute. I'll need fresh lipstick if we're going out in public."

The washroom door clicked closed, and Tom settled back with the fudge. He had consulted his notebook while talking to Mrs. Ruggles, and now he flipped through the pages, checking details. Realizing he'd forgotten to make a note on the cigarette butt, he took the envelope from his pocket and copied out the details.

"What's that?" Mrs. Ruggles asked, returning from the washroom.

"Oh, I thought this was a clue," Tom answered, ripping open the envelope and removing the butt. "I found it in Bedroom C."

"A clue?"

"Well, the killer might have left it behind by mistake." Smiling, Tom pointed at the red smear on the butt. "However, I don't think Mr. Faith wears lipstick."

Mrs. Ruggles laughed. "I hope not."

"I tried to make out the brand name of the cigarette, but this lipstick stain covers most of it. Anyway, it's obvious Catherine Saks left it in the ashtray." Tom thought back to the beautiful woman at the breakfast table, looking so elegant with the long cigarette holder in her fingers. Then, with a shock, he thought of something.

"Hey!" he said, staring at the butt.

"What?" Mrs. Ruggles asked.

"Hey, just a minute. Catherine Saks used a cigarette holder, which means her cigarettes never touched her lips. So this lipstick stain can't be hers."

"That doesn't make sense, Tom," Mrs. Ruggles said, sitting down in her chair and picking up her handbag from the floor.

"Sure it does!" Tom said, excited. "Some other woman was in her bedroom that night, smoking."

Mrs. Ruggles laughed. "Really, Tom, that is far-fetched. If you want me to help with your case, you'll need to have better theories."

"You don't understand," Tom said, impatient that the old lady's mind worked so slowly. He was trying to think of another way to explain about the lipstick, when his eyes fell on one of her butts still smouldering in the ashtray. "You'd better put that out," he said.

102 | ERIC WILSON

"Oh, yes."

Mrs. Ruggles reached for the butt, and ground it firmly out. As she did, Tom realized that it had a red lipstick stain. A cold, sick feeling spread through his body as he lifted his eyes to stare at Mrs. Ruggles.

Smiling, the old lady reached one hand to her head and lifted off her wig, revealing thick black hair which shone in the light from the window. At the same moment, she took a small revolver from her handbag and pointed it at Tom.

"Congratulations," she said. "You just found the killer."

9

"I don't understand," Tom said, feeling sad and stupid.

Mrs. Ruggles returned the wig to her head, adjusting it carefully. "A few more hours and I'd have been safely off the train," she said, her voice no longer that of an old woman. "I didn't figure on a kid wrecking my plans."

A million thoughts tumbled inside Tom's head, surprise, foolishness, despair. Fear of the black revolver which pointed straight at his heart. He had found the killer, and he was trapped.

"Why you?" Tom said unhappily. "I like you."

Mrs. Ruggles smiled. "And I like you. You did okay, solving this case."

"Are you going to kill me?"

"Only if necessary."

Tom stared at the revolver, wondering if he should throw himself at the old lady and wrestle with her for it. But she wasn't an old lady, and she had already killed one person.

"Who are you?" he asked.

"Be quiet, while I think," Mrs. Ruggles said. There was a long silence, then she nodded her head. "Yes, that's a good plan."

"Who are you?" Tom repeated.

"I'm the cashier from the bank."

"What?" Tom said, surprised.

"Mr. Faith was right, when he suspected Richard Saks had framed me for the robbery." Mrs. Ruggles leaned toward Tom. "But it wasn't Richard's fault, it was that rotten Catherine. She made him do it."

"Were you with her in Hollywood?"

"Yes, we went there together to become stars, but Catherine couldn't act. She got sick of trying to succeed, and insisted that we return to Winnipeg. She always got her own way, so we came home and found jobs at Richard's bank. Before long, we were both in love with Richard." Mrs. Ruggles smiled, but her mouth was bitter. "Guess who got him?"

Tom remembered the way Catherine Saks had treated her husband at the breakfast table. "She didn't seem to be in love."

"It didn't last long." Mrs. Ruggles looked down sadly, and for a second the gun wavered in her hand. "All she wanted from Richard was money, so she forced him to steal from the bank. I knew about it, but I didn't say anything, because I loved Richard."

"Do you still love him?"

"Yes, but I wanted revenge, especially against Catherine. When I read in the newspaper they were taking this trip, I planned the perfect murder."

Mrs. Ruggles seemed to have forgotten the gun, and it drooped lower and lower as she spoke. "Two weeks ago I terrified Catherine by phoning her to warn I wanted revenge. Then, to avoid suspicion, I went to Brandon and boarded the train acting my role of little old lady."

Mrs. Ruggles paused, looking pleased.

"Catherine never recognized me. Last night, after she fought with Richard in the bar, I followed her to their bedroom and offered a sympathetic ear. Catherine told me all her woes, and then I gave her a piece of fudge."

"Filled with cyanide," Tom said, shivering.

Mrs. Ruggles nodded. "She popped it in her mouth, and started chewing. As she did, I took off my wig and smiled at her. Catherine used to say I was a poor actor, but she didn't think that as she died."

Tom stared at the woman, realizing what a vicious person was masked by the make-up and wig.

"When she was dead, I stabbed her body and went to my bedroom. When I heard Richard return, I raised the alarm, pretending I'd heard a fight."

By now the revolver was almost pointing at the floor. Gathering courage, Tom thought of another question to keep Mrs. Ruggles talking. "If you loved Richard Saks, how could you set him up for a murder rap?"

"I just wanted him to have a taste of what I went through. When they get Catherine's body to a city, they'll find the cyanide and fudge in her stomach and know Richard wasn't the killer. By then old Mrs. Ruggles will be off the train and gone forever."

No you won't, Tom thought. He bunched his muscles to spring at the woman, but there was a knock at the door and the gun snapped up.

"Who's there?" Mrs. Ruggles called in her old lady's voice.

"Porter, ma'am. Shall I bring you some tea?"

"Not this afternoon, thank you."

"Everything fine?"

"Hunky-dory," Mrs. Ruggles said, smiling at Tom. "A young man has come by for some fudge."

"Have fun, then," the porter called.

Fudge. Tom felt sick, realizing how easily he might have been poisoned. His detective work had landed him in a real mess, and there was no way out.

"And now," Mrs. Ruggles said, "it's time to eliminate young Tom Austen."

"You wouldn't shoot me," Tom said, trying to sound tough.

"Want a bet?"

Keeping the gun aimed at Tom, Mrs. Ruggles leaned close to the window and looked toward the front of the train. "Good," she said, "here's a chance now."

"You won't get away with this," Tom said. "Give yourself up to the police."

Mrs. Ruggles laughed. "You sound like a TV show. Now listen carefully, sonny. We're going to leave the bedroom and walk to the end of the sleeping-car. I'll have the gun under my shawl, and if anything goes wrong I'll kill you."

"If you do, you'll go to prison."

"You forget I've already killed. One more corpse won't make any difference."

Tom trembled, remembering the grey blanket which had covered Catherine Saks when her body was taken away. He'd better obey, or he too would leave the train feet first.

"Open the door."

Tom did as ordered, hoping foolishly that a dozen Mounties would be waiting outside to ambush Mrs. Ruggles, but the corridor was empty and silent except for the lonely clack-clack of the wheels.

"Quickly," Mrs. Ruggles said, poking Tom in the back with her cane.

They hurried down the corridor and past the roomettes without seeing anyone. As they stepped into the vestibule between the cars, Tom looked out the window and saw darkness. For a confused second he thought it was night, then realized the train was inside a tunnel.

"Open the outside door," Mrs. Ruggles said.

Tom was beginning to understand what she planned. He looked at the woman, hoping for sympathy, but the cold look in her eyes showed he must obey. He unlatched the door and swung it open, hearing the sounds of the train magnified by the tunnel.

"Now the floor panel," Mrs. Ruggles said above the noise.

Tom lifted it away, and the steel steps lay waiting. "Hurry up," Mrs. Ruggles said, pushing Tom with her cane. "Go to the bottom, and jump."

Tom started down slowly, the diesel fumes filling his nose. He reached the bottom step and looked out fearfully, knowing the train was moving slowly but afraid to step into darkness.

"Jump," Mrs. Ruggles called.

Tom turned, and looked up at the woman. "I can't," he whispered. "I'm afraid."

"Do as I say!" Mrs. Ruggles said angrily, leaning forward to poke Tom with her cane.

Fear was tight in Tom's throat. "I can't jump," he said, dodging the cane.

"You must!" Mrs. Ruggles came down two steps, trying to shove Tom out the door, but he kept jumping away from her cane.

The woman came down one more step, leaned forward, and pushed Tom with her hand. As she did, Tom threw up his arm in self-defence and his fingers tangled in her shawl; he toppled backwards clutching the shawl, and the two figures fell together out of the train.

Metal burned into Tom's back, his head hit

something, and a roar filled his ears. He gasped for air, sure that he was dying, then opened his eyes and saw the dim shape of the train's wheels rolling past.

Tom turned his head, feeling it throb, and saw Mrs. Ruggles lying on her back. He sat up painfully and crawled to her side, hoping to find the gun, but her eyes opened and she grabbed his arm. As she did, the last car of the train went past and its lights faded away down the tunnel.

Now there was only silence and darkness.

Tom tried to pull away from the woman's hand, but her grip was firm. He could hear the sound of her breathing, but saw nothing.

"I've got my gun," Mrs. Ruggles whispered. "Give me one excuse, and I'll gladly kill you."

Tom was silent, not wanting his voice to reveal his fear. The woman's strong grip hurt, and the rocks of the tunnel floor were cutting into his knees, but he could only think of escaping the cold, damp air which choked around his head.

"Help me get up," Mrs. Ruggles said.

The silk of her old dress rustled as she stood up, leaning heavily on Tom's shoulder, then pulled him to his feet.

"This is all your fault," the woman's voice said angrily. "When we're out of this tunnel, I'm going to get rid of you for good."

Tom listened to the terrifying words echo inside the tunnel, knowing he must act now to save his life. Without warning, he kicked out and felt his shoe connect with the woman's leg. She cried out with pain, and her grip loosened; with a quick motion Tom tore free, turned, and ran.

"Come back!" Mrs. Ruggles shouted.

There was a red flash, followed by a loud bang, and a bullet crashed against the tunnel wall. Tom stopped running, realizing she had shot toward the sound of his feet, and stood waiting in fear. The black air was silent while long seconds passed.

Then, he heard footsteps.

Mrs. Ruggles was coming slowly in his direction. Tom heard her feet stepping cautiously as she worked her way forward in the darkness. His heart thumping, he bent down for a rock, and threw it in her direction.

For a moment he heard nothing, then the rock smacked against the tunnel wall. Mrs. Ruggles shouted in surprise and fired toward the sound, the flash and roar of the gun huge inside the tunnel.

Again, silence spread through the darkness. Tom listened, waiting for movement, and at last heard the woman's cautious footsteps. Closer they came, the rocks crunching under her feet, until she was so close that Tom could hear her harsh breathing.

Every muscle in his body was rigid with fear as the feet went past. They walked on into the darkness, and suddenly stopped.

The railway tracks were humming.

Tom turned his head, listening to the strange sound which quivered in the rails, then heard a distant rattle. It hung in the black air, died, and came again. The hum grew louder, and a dim glow began to melt the black air. Somewhere far down the tunnel, still out of sight but coming this way, was a light, its beam gradually pushing aside the darkness which surrounded Tom and Mrs. Ruggles. Very soon she would see where he was standing, and shoot.

Tom leaned over and picked up a rock in each hand. He looked toward the darkness where he had last heard footsteps, drew back his arm, and threw.

The rock clattered against the tunnel wall, and the gun roared.

With all his energy, Tom threw the second rock toward the place where he had seen the gun's flash.

This time there was a cry of pain; Tom turned, and was running toward the distant glow when he heard a bang and the sound of a bullet.

Tom put down his head and ran faster. The light was close now, glowing in the darkness ahead, and he could hear the sound of a motor. Seconds later, a headlight burst around a distant bend.

Gasping for breath, Tom threw himself forward. As the headlight grew stronger, he raised his arms to wave, and heard the rasp of steel against steel as brakes were applied.

"Who are you?" a man's voice shouted.

Tom shielded his eyes against the headlight and ran toward the voice. When he was past the glare, he saw two men sitting in a railway scooter piled high with repair tools. Thrilled to see them, Tom raised a shaking hand and pointed down the tunnel.

"Please help me!" he said. " There's a woman with a gun."

The men looked at each other. "I told you those were shots," one said.

The second man reached down to Tom. "Climb aboard," he said, helping Tom into the scooter.

"She'll shoot," Tom warned. "Be careful."

The scooter started forward, its headlight gleaming along the rails. At first there was no sign of Mrs. Ruggles, but then Tom saw a distant figure, running.

"There she is!" he shouted.

The scooter picked up speed, the throb of its motor echoing around their ears. As they closed in on Mrs. Ruggles, she fired a shot over her shoulder, but the bullet went wide of the scooter. Stopping to aim, she squeezed the trigger again, but nothing happened. Once more the woman tried, then threw the empty gun in their direction.

It smacked against the front of the scooter and clattered to the tunnel floor. Mrs. Ruggles turned to run, but one man was already out of the scooter and managed to catch her arm. She struggled desperately, but the man twisted her arm painfully behind her back and led her to the scooter.

Mrs. Ruggles looked at Tom and held up a bleeding hand. "You hit me with a rock," she said, almost crying. "How could you do that, when you said you liked me?"

There was no way Tom could answer her question.

10

Mrs. Ruggles was bundled into the scooter, and it rolled quickly out of the tunnel and along the tracks to the next station. From there, the police were called and a message radioed ahead for *The Canadian* to be stopped.

Once Tom had given a statement to the Mounties and watched Mrs. Ruggles being driven away under guard, the scooter crew gave him a ride to the waiting train, which had stopped on a siding overlooking a green lake surrounded by mountains.

Some of the passengers had left the train to stretch their legs and take pictures of the scenery. Rumours had already begun to spread about Tom and Mrs. Ruggles, and the scooter was surrounded by curious faces the moment it stopped.

"What happened?" Dietmar asked, shoving through the crowd to stare at Tom.

"Nothing much," Tom answered. "I fell out of the train, and these guys gave me a lift back."

But such modesty did not apply to the scooter crew, one of whom stood up and looked around at the crowd. "This kid and us are heroes!" he said proudly. "We just caught a murderer."

"Who?" someone asked, and other voices joined in: "Where? Why? When?"

"Just a minute!" It was the conductor, pushing through the passengers. "Everybody climb on board, so the train can get moving. Then you can all gather in the dining-car, and let this young fellow tell what happened."

Inside the train the smiling steward provided refreshments and Tom told his story to the people who crowded into the dining-car. Then, questions were asked to fill in the blanks.

"Did you have any idea that Mrs. Ruggles had murdered Catherine Saks?" one man asked.

"No," Tom admitted, "but there were several clues which should have told me she was the killer."

"What were they?"

"First, there was the cigarette butt with the red lipstick stain. Because of Catherine Saks's cigarette holder, I should have realized another woman had been in Bedroom C."

Tom paused for a drink of pop.

"During bingo Mrs. Ruggles mentioned that Catherine Saks had five lines in one movie. Why would she know the exact details of a stranger's movie career? That was a tip-off I missed, plus it was odd that Mrs. Ruggles didn't have any pictures of the grandchildren she claimed to be going to visit. Most grandparents carry at least a dozen pictures of beaming babies."

Mr. Faith raised his hand to ask a question. "Were there any clues to indicate the killer was a woman?"

"Yes," Tom said. "At the breakfast table I learned that Catherine Saks worked at the bank with a friend. Later, you told me that Richard Saks was thought to have framed a cashier at his bank. I already suspected that someone wanted Richard Saks to look guilty of murder, so I should have realized it was the cashier who'd done it for revenge."

As Tom spoke, the train's speed dropped and it entered a tunnel. Even though he knew he was safe, Tom shivered as he looked out at the darkness.

"You know," he said, "it's too bad she didn't stay in Hollywood, because she was a really good actor."

"She fooled us all," Mr. Faith said. "With that rouge and powder covering her skin, I never realized she might be a young woman."

Someone was tugging at Tom's sleeve. He looked down, and saw the cookie-woman sitting at a table with her tin of goodies open. "Have one of these," she said, smiling. "I think you're a fine young man."

"Thanks," Tom said, selecting a large chocolate-chip cookie. "By the way, did I mention that you were a suspect?"

"Me?" the woman said, annoyed.

"Yes," Tom said, quickly gulping the cookie before the woman could ask for it back. "I thought you might have given Catherine Saks a cookie laced with cyanide. Of course you hadn't, but I should have remembered that Mrs. Ruggles was passing around fudge, which could also contain poison."

The woman turned to her husband. "Imagine," she said, "thinking my cookies would kill someone."

This produced a laugh from the other passengers, and even the cookie-woman's brittle face broke into a smile when she realized how foolish she sounded. Some people got up to leave, and others came forward to shake Tom's hand.

Among them was the little boy in the baseball cap. "Congratulations, mister," he said, holding out his hand.

Too late, Tom saw the water pistol. The boy fired a deadly stream into Tom's face and turned to run, but this time Tom reached out quickly and caught his collar.

"Come here," he said, leading the squirming boy into the empty corridor.

When Tom reappeared he was smiling, but the little boy didn't look as if he'd been damaged. More passengers swirled around, patting Tom's back and calling him a fine specimen of humanity, and then he spotted Mr. Faith about to leave the car.

"Mr. Faith!" he called, pushing through the passengers. "Just a minute!"

"Yes?" the man said, pausing by the door.

"Please open your attaché case and show me what's inside."

"I can't do that," the man said, but other people were crowding around, and a woman suggested he open it as a reward for Tom. Reluctantly agreeing, Mr. Faith shielded the case's combination lock and spun the dial.

"I can't wait to see this," Tom said, leaning close. "I bet it's full of diamonds and rubies."

But Tom was wrong, for all he could see inside was a stack of paper. He looked up at Mr. Faith, disappointed.

"I knew you didn't believe me," the man said. "No one believes in me."

"I don't get it."

"I'm a writer. This is my latest manuscript, which I'm taking to a publisher in Vancouver."

"But how can it be worth a million dollars?"

"Arthur Hailey made a million dollars for his book, *Airport*. With luck, I'll do the same with this book."

"What's it called?" someone asked.

"Oh no you don't." Mr. Faith closed the lid of the attaché case. "No one is going to get my title."

"Why do you have the case locked to your wrist?" Tom asked, pointing at the handcuffs.

"All Hemingway's early manuscripts were stolen in a railway station," Mr. Faith said. "That will never happen to me."

"Boy," Tom said, "I've never met a writer before. I'll be watching for your book to come out."

Mr. Faith looked pleased. "I've already had some paperbacks published, under the pen names William Hope and Robert Charity. Why don't you buy those, too?"

"Hey!" Tom said, snapping his fingers. "I'll bet you've got another pen name."

"What?"

"Franklin W. Dixon!"

"Never heard of him."

"Oh," Tom said, surprised. "It's strange that you haven't, because he's the greatest. He writes the Hardy Boys stories."

"What are they about?"

Tom stared at Mr. Faith, shocked at his ignorance. "About two brothers who are detectives. You see their books everywhere."

"Do you?" Mr. Faith looked interested, and studied Tom carefully. "You're quite a detective yourself. Maybe I'll write a book about you, and earn a million dollars."

Tom grinned. " That would be great!"

"On second thought," Mr. Faith said, "I don't think it would make any money. Let's forget it."

Tom was disappointed, but didn't let it show. He was about to turn away when a man with red hair and a beard spoke up from a corner of the crowd.

"I'll write about you," he said to Tom. "You'll be the most famous character since Puck of Pook's Hill."

Everyone laughed, including Tom. "One final thing," he said to Mr. Faith. "Why did you desert me in that town? I almost missed the train."

"I got tired of your questions. Anyway, trains are like girlfriends. If you miss one, there'll be another along soon."

Picking up his attaché case, Mr. Faith left the dining-car. As the other passengers began to drift away, Tom saw Dietmar standing by a table, picking at cake crumbs on a plate.

"Still hungry?" Tom said, walking over. "Would you like a stick of gum?"

Dietmar nodded. "Okay."

"You know," Tom said, as he held out the package to Dietmar, "I never forgot that bomb trick you played on me."

"Poor Tom," Dietmar said, laughing. And then, he pulled the gum out of the package . . .

About the Author

Eric Wilson was born in Ottawa and grew up in communities from coast to coast. His Dad's work with the RCMP took the Wilson family to many places, so Eric really got to know and love Canada. His boyhood dream was to write exciting mysteries about real Canadian settings.